PRAISE F̶.̶ ̶ ̶ ̶ ̶ ̶.̶ ̶ ̶ ̶ ̶ ̶ ̶ ̶AN

Tom Clancy fans open to a strong female lead will clamor for more.

— *DRONE*, PUBLISHERS WEEKLY

Superb!

— *DRONE*, BOOKLIST STARRED REVIEW

The best military thriller I've read in a very long time. Love the female characters.

— *DRONE,* SHELDON MCARTHUR, FOUNDER OF THE MYSTERY BOOKSTORE, LA

A fabulous soaring thriller.

— *TAKE OVER AT MIDNIGHT,* MIDWEST BOOK REVIEW

Meticulously researched, hard-hitting, and suspenseful.

— *PURE HEAT,* PUBLISHERS WEEKLY, STARRED REVIEW

Expert technical details abound, as do realistic military missions with superb imagery that will have readers feeling as if they are right there in the midst and on the edges of their seats.

Buchman has catapulted his way to the top tier of my favorite authors.

Nonstop action that will keep readers on the edge of their seats.

M L. Buchman's ability to keep the reader right in the middle of the action is amazing.

The only thing you'll ask yourself is, "When does the next one come out?"

The first...of (a) stellar, long-running (military) romantic suspense series.

— *THE NIGHT IS MINE,* BOOKLIST, "THE 20 BEST ROMANTIC SUSPENSE NOVELS: MODERN MASTERPIECES"

I knew the books would be good, but I didn't realize how good.

— NIGHT STALKERS SERIES, KIRKUS REVIEWS

Buchman mixes adrenalin-spiking battles and brusque military jargon with a sensitive approach.

— PUBLISHERS WEEKLY

13 times "Top Pick of the Month"

— NIGHT OWL REVIEWS

AT THE CLEAREST SENSATION

A PARANORMAL ROMANTIC SUSPENSE

M. L. BUCHMAN

Buchman Bookworks

Other works by M. L. Buchman: *(* - also in audio)*

Thrillers

Dead Chef
Swap Out!
One Chef!
Two Chef!

Miranda Chase
Drone*
Thunderbolt*
Condor*

Romantic Suspense

Delta Force
Target Engaged*
Heart Strike*
Wild Justice*
Midnight Trust*

Firehawks
MAIN FLIGHT
Pure Heat
Full Blaze
Hot Point*
Flash of Fire*
Wild Fire
SMOKEJUMPERS
Wildfire at Dawn*
Wildfire at Larch Creek*
Wildfire on the Skagit*

The Night Stalkers
MAIN FLIGHT
The Night Is Mine
I Own the Dawn
Wait Until Dark
Take Over at Midnight
Light Up the Night
Bring On the Dusk
By Break of Day

AND THE NAVY
Christmas at Steel Beach
Christmas at Peleliu Cove
WHITE HOUSE HOLIDAY
Daniel's Christmas*
Frank's Independence Day*
Peter's Christmas*
Zachary's Christmas*
Roy's Independence Day*
Damien's Christmas*
5E
Target of the Heart
Target Lock on Love
Target of Mine
Target of One's Own

Shadow Force: Psi
At the Slightest Sound*
At the Quietest Word*

White House Protection Force
Off the Leash*
On Your Mark*
In the Weeds*

Contemporary Romance

Eagle Cove
Return to Eagle Cove
Recipe for Eagle Cove
Longing for Eagle Cove
Keepsake for Eagle Cove

Henderson's Ranch
Nathan's Big Sky*
Big Sky, Loyal Heart*
Big Sky Dog Whisperer*

Love Abroad
Heart of the Cotswolds: England
Path of Love: Cinque Terre, Italy

Other works by M. L. Buchman:

Contemporary Romance (cont)

Where Dreams
Where Dreams are Born
Where Dreams Reside
Where Dreams Are of Christmas
Where Dreams Unfold
Where Dreams Are Written

Science Fiction / Fantasy

Deities Anonymous
Cookbook from Hell: Reheated
Saviors 101

Single Titles
The Nara Reaction
Monk's Maze
the Me and Elsie Chronicles

Non-Fiction

Strategies for Success
Managing Your Inner Artist/Writer
Estate Planning for Authors*
Character Voice
Narrate and Record Your Own
Audiobook*

Short Story Series by M. L. Buchman:

Romantic Suspense

Delta Force
Delta Force

Firehawks
The Firehawks Lookouts
The Firehawks Hotshots
The Firebirds

The Night Stalkers
The Night Stalkers
The Night Stalkers 5E
The Night Stalkers CSAR
The Night Stalkers Wedding Stories

US Coast Guard
US Coast Guard

White House Protection Force
White House Protection Force

Contemporary Romance

Eagle Cove
Eagle Cove

Henderson's Ranch
Henderson's Ranch*

Where Dreams
Where Dreams

Thrillers

Dead Chef
Dead Chef

Science Fiction / Fantasy

Deities Anonymous
Deities Anonymous

Other
The Future Night Stalkers
Single Titles

ABOUT THIS BOOK

Hollywood star Isobel Manella leads a charmed life in many ways: interesting roles, surrounded by friends and family, and the ability to sense precisely what those around her are feeling. Her empathic skills help her and her team shine.

Sailor and film handyman Devlin Jones enjoys the job niche he's created along Seattle's waterfront. His skills as a Jack of all trades keeps him fed, companionship can always be found, and his beloved Dragon sailboat lies moored just outside his back door.

However, when Devlin takes Isobel on an evening sail, he brings aboard far more trouble than he's ever faced before. As an assistant on her upcoming film, he thought he could just sail through the gig. Little did he know she'd completely change the uncharted course of his future.

CHAPTER 1

*I*sobel Manella stood at the end of her pier. Sadly, she was there in both the literal and metaphorical sense. The film actress in her appreciated the juxtaposition, but the woman she was didn't at all. Except it wasn't even a dramatic pier, it was just a little floating dock, and the crashing waves were inch-high wind ripples rolling across the quiet urban lake to lap below her feet.

"What was I thinking?"

The gull bobbing gently nearby didn't answer back and she really, really wished it would.

Reflecting the Seattle skyline, Lake Union lay quiet beneath the summer sunset. The breeze rippled the surface just enough to break up the bright reflection of the lowering sun. It was hard to believe that she was in the heart of a major American city. Her home in San Antonio might boast the River Walk, but it had nothing like this.

The lake was a half-mile wide and a mile-and-a-half long. The southern shore was protected from the urban core by a thin line of restaurants and a wooden boat museum. The expanse of a park filled the north end with a lovely grassy hill that caught the evening light.

To the east and west, tall hills rose steeply, thick with a piney green so verdant that it practically clogged the air with oxygen. Only scattered apartment blocks and low office buildings risked those slopes that resisted most attempts at urbanization.

On this quiet June Tuesday, the lake was thick with more sailboats than all of Canyon Lake on July 4th weekend. Every year, Mama had made a point of driving the forty miles from San Antonio to take her and Ricardo there for the parade and fireworks. After she'd died, they'd only gone one more time —to scatter her ashes where their father's had been all these years.

Isobel had never become attached to the sea; it was too vast and unruly. But she loved the happy bustle of a big lake.

The shoreline here was lined with marinas for boats of all sizes from daysailers to mega-yachts. Even a few massive workboats added their contrast to the scenery.

Several large houseboat communities also gathered along the shore. Though houseboats conjured the wrong image for her. A houseboat was a trailer on a rectangular metal hull rented for a few days on Canyon Lake. These were actual floating homes, hovering along finger piers that stuck out from the shore. They created a world away from the city, a quiet corner, without having to travel miles through sprawling suburbs to seek some peace. From here, the predominant evening sounds were the slapping of sails interrupted by the occasional hard burr of a seaplane lifting from the water.

No, the problem wasn't the lake. Or the "houseboat" she'd rented for the team. She turned to look at it, a pleasingly eclectic mix of old and new. The weathered cedar-shake siding was offset by the dramatically large windows.

It had four bedrooms, three baths, and a luxurious great room that spanned the entire first floor and made it easy for her team to all be together or spread out in smaller groups. It had an open plan kitchen that reminded her how much she used to enjoy cooking, back when she had the time.

The back deck had a rack of single and double kayaks. A smaller deck spanned across the two front bedrooms on the second story. And the rooftop deck was ideal for looking out over the lake to watch the sunset light up the sixty-story-high Space Needle even though the sun would soon be sliding off the lake and going behind Queen Anne hill.

She could happily stay here forever.

Another spatter of laughter sounded from the rooftop deck, which she could hear clearly from where she'd "reached the end of her dock."

The problem was her team.

Not that she didn't love them all.

But the other members of Shadow Force: Psi were now three couples. Her twin brother had married Isobel's best friend. They now supported each other more than her. She wouldn't wish it otherwise, but still she missed them—even though they were right …there, up on the roof. And her best friend's stepbrother had just become engaged to a lovely English lass. Even the quiet Hannah and her cowboy husband were utterly charming.

But she could *feel* their happiness.

She and Ricardo had grown up in a hard household. Papa dead in the Gulf War. Mama a single mother who'd run an entire nursing staff at a major hospital. Isobel had run their household from the time she could reach the stovetop from a stool.

They'd made it. A tight, hard-working unit. Then, while Isobel was in college and Ricardo in the Army, Mama was

3

suddenly gone. Her death still left a hole in Isobel's heart that the last decade had proved would never heal.

By keeping her team close, she was surrounded by happiness every day.

Yet she wasn't just a third wheel to Ricardo and Michelle's happiness. She was now a seventh wheel to all three couples.

Shadow Force: Psi was between missions, so they'd all accompanied her here and were looking forward to helping on her latest film—with an excitement that was a little overwhelming. They'd arrived in Seattle just this morning and everyone had plunged into enjoying themselves as not a one of the others had been here before. Nine years and a lifetime ago she'd been here to shoot her breakout rom-com but not been back since.

Isobel had been managing it, enjoying their sense of fun.

Until Michelle had announced that she was pregnant.

The general excitement had turned to near ecstatic joy. Hannah had exchanged a look with Jesse, who then announced that they were going to start trying, too. Michelle had cried on Hannah's shoulder that she might not be facing this alone—as if that was possible in this group.

Isobel couldn't be happier for them...but her mind couldn't shut them out.

They each had their unique gifts. Some of them could switch them on and off, others couldn't. Michelle and Ricardo shared a telepathic link that was unique to them, and always worked without fail. Though Ricardo occasionally complained about being unable to shut out his wife's thoughts. The others had absolute control over their skills. Hannah and Jessie could do strange things with creating sounds, really strange and useful things if they were in physical contact. Michelle's stepbrother Anton could send his vision out to take a look around without having to drag his body along. And his fiancée Katie could feel if someone had been in a certain spot and then use her wilderness tracking skills to follow their trail.

Normally, her own empathic gift was wholly under her control. She could choose to sense what those around her were truly feeling, or she could shut them out and just be "normal."

It was a skill she'd always had, but hadn't known was unusual until Papa had been killed in action. Mama had put on the brave mask for her four-year-old children, but Isobel had been overwhelmed by that hidden grief. She'd had to learn at a very early age how to turn off her extra sense in order to survive.

But tonight the joy was so thick in the air, she hadn't been able to shut it out. She couldn't breathe.

"How can we stand it?" she asked the gull who had drifted to the other side of the dock.

Apparently deciding that she couldn't (or that Isobel was not being sufficiently forthcoming with some torn bread), the gull fluttered aloft and soared off in search of less frustrating places.

If only she could do the same.

Again happy laughter, big and deep this time. It sounded as if Michelle's stepbrother, Anton, had talked Katie into *all* of them trying to have their children close together even though their own wedding was a month off.

Isobel rubbed her own midriff.

She ached to be like them. Be one of them in this moment.

But all she could see of the future was becoming Auntie Isobel. Always cheering for others but never for herself.

Her face had been on every cover from *Vogue* to *The Hollywood Reporter* as her career had exploded. Even her Christmas blockbuster had busted the block beyond all projections. *People* had imaginatively dubbed her "The Sun-kissed Actress." No matter how non-PC it was to emphasize her skin color, it was true that fortune was absolutely smiling down on her. Amazing career. Incredible friends who truly understood the joys and fears of being gifted. A challenging life with the secretive Shadow Force.

And the personal life of a lone oyster. At least those lucky mollusks got pearls.

Every man who saw her instantly thought he knew her—and wanted to conquer her. Not her, but rather her-the Movie Star. Her chances of finding what all of her friends up above were now celebrating decreased with each passing film.

The evening was still bright, but soon the team would notice she was gone.

Michelle would come find her first; she knew Isobel's moods better than Isobel did herself. She'd slip a friendly arm around Isobel's waist—her emotions thick with the green velvet of her core kindness, and rolling pink with compassion—and say something completely outrageous that would make her laugh and feel as if she belonged and was just being foolish.

Isobel didn't want to be consoled. She didn't want to live through her friends' relationships, through *their* children.

Since playing the "Crippled Girl" in *The Pied Piper of Hamlin* during second grade—a role she'd landed because her mother the nurse had been able to borrow a child-sized crutch from the hospital—she'd loved acting. But the price! The price was terribly high, and growing all the time.

She closed her eyes and concentrated on shutting herself off from others.

There was only her, the evening breeze, the warmth of the early evening sun on her face. She leaned toward its warmth. She could just—

"Don't do it!"

Isobel opened her eyes and looked at the man who'd called out to her. He floated a short way off in an elegant sailboat. It was long and lean, with a teak deck and a bright-varnished wooden hull. She'd never sailed on one, but she knew it was a model called a Dragon. It had been easy to remember because it was how sleek a flying serpent should look.

"Excuse me?"

"Don't jump, lady. Whatever's wrong, it's not worth it."

She looked down at the water lapping quietly a foot below her bare toes. One of the first things they'd all done on arrival this afternoon was jump into the water and swim about to wash off the flight from San Antonio.

"I *think* I'd survive the fall."

"Maybe there's a hungry Kraken lurking below. Why risk possible doom when you can sail?"

She focused on the man. His skin was roughly as dark as her own though differently toned—less Latin-brown, more desert ochre. Black hair strayed down to his collar and a close-trimmed beard and mustache emphasized the strong cheekbones that stood out despite his mirrored sunglasses. He wore denim cutoffs, and the edge of a colorful tattoo peeked out from the sleeve of a white t-shirt that declared, "I'd rather be sailing."

She nodded toward his t-shirt. "But you are sailing."

"Wouldn't *you* rather be sailing?"

"I'd rather be doing *anything*."

With a casual ease that showed long practice, he slipped the pretty boat from drifting to sidling up to the dock.

A quick touch with her empathic powers and she sensed no lust or avarice, which was good enough for her. Besides, the lake was small enough that if he got strange, she could always dive overboard and swim ashore. Then maybe the

Kraken would come, swallow her whole, and that would solve everything.

Timing her moment, she stepped aboard and settled in a seat. He didn't offer a hand, which she appreciated. She was a competent enough sailor to manage herself on a boat.

She'd had to be for the storm scene in that long-ago breakout rom-com *Where Dreams Sail*. They'd gone out to film on a prediction of twenty knots, and gotten caught in gale that gusted to forty—over fifty miles an hour—out in the Straits of San Juan de Fuca.

Isobel avoided stunt doubles whenever possible. It was in her contracts that it was always up to her. No one, not the director or the insurance company, could keep her from doing what she felt an actress needed to do. If it took an extra month of sailing lessons to do it safely, then that was her problem, not theirs.

That storm had launched her career from just another rom-com love interest into the kick-ass heroine stratosphere. During filming, she'd been too busy staying alive to be scared—until she saw the footage they'd managed to capture. That was still her craziest stunt yet.

As silently as the wind, the sleek boat slipped away from the dock, the houseboat, and her friends' happy chatter.

She managed to resist the temptation to see if her team had noted her departure.

As the light evening breeze—no gales tonight—filled the sail, the boat launched ahead.

~

Devlin had planned on running solo for the Tuesday evening Duck Dodge race. He generally preferred it that way. If he was dating someone, he might invite them along—but he might not. Even in the madness of a hundred boats gathering for a completely foolish race, he liked being just a man and his boat.

But something about the lady on the dock in a fluttering sundress the color of spring had made him swing over. She'd made a breathtaking image. Long dark hair curling down past her shoulders. Serious curves. He'd always been a fan of curves on a woman. She'd looked like a Latina Madonna.

The sadness had practically radiated off her, which simply wasn't right for such a lovely evening. Despite that, she'd kept her sense of humor. He liked that in a woman even more than he liked serious curves.

"Do you sail?"

"I do, though it's been a while." Damn but the woman had a voice. Smooth Mexican-lilted Texan.

"It's like a bicycle. Care to take over the jib sheets?" They crossed from the sunlight eastern edge of the lake to the shadowed western side below Queen Anne. She'd had no jacket, but the air was warm and she made no comment. Which was good, as he hadn't even thought to toss a slick down below.

She didn't even hesitate as she shifted sides and prewrapped the windward jib sheet around the high-side winch without having to be told that a sheet was a sailor's word for a line used to trim a sail. With her fine-fingered hand, she tapped the winch handle resting in its holding sleeve. He'd wager that now she could grab it blind.

"You have a name, lady?" He checked local traffic.

The summer Duck Dodge series involved around a hundred sailboats every Tuesday evening. They ranged from dinghies to ninety-foot schooners and all levels of skill. He'd spent too many hours buffing his boat's hull to go bouncing it off some weekend sailor-wanna-be.

He could feel her watching him but there was a Cal 26

that was worrying him at the moment and he didn't dare look away.

"Belle," her voice sounded unsure. "My name is Belle."

"Ready to come about," he warned her.

He didn't really need to tack yet, but her studying gaze was actually a little unnerving.

She finally looked away, took the long tail of the windward sheet in one hand, and shifted to where she could release the leeward sheet. "Ready about."

The way she said it finally made the connection click.

He wasn't a big movie guy, but a sailing movie set in Seattle? No way to resist that. And *Where Dreams Sail* had starred the young and sultry Isobel Manella—*my name is Belle*. She'd been so out of place, sad on a Lake Union dock, that he hadn't recognized her despite having gone to see that movie a couple of times, paying real money instead of waiting for it to hit the tube. Then he'd bought the damned DVD. But that sure as hell didn't seem like a conversation she needed tonight. That explained the sudden tension in her voice.

"Belle, huh? I guess that makes me The Beast."

"It might. The jury is still out on that," she answered more easily.

He'd just picked up one of the most famous movie stars anywhere. Well, if she didn't want to be recognized, he was okay with that.

"Are we coming about anytime soon?" She directed his attention back to the pre-race antics as everyone maneuvered for position near the starting line.

"Sure, why not." Especially if he didn't want to ram Hank's committee boat. "Helm's alee," and he shoved the tiller to the leeward side.

She waited until the foresail had backed slightly, accelerating the speed with which the bow crossed through the wind and over to the opposite tack. Then she freed the line, and with timing he couldn't fault, hauled in the other sheet quickly, catching an extra loop on the winch before the sail could fully draw. Glancing up at the sail and wind once he settled on the new tack, she took two quick turns on the winch, checked aloft once more, and took one more turn before dropping the handle back in its sleeve.

"Belle knows her boats."

In answer she prepped the other sheet for the next tack, then shot him a million-watt smile. Jesus, talk about a screen dazzler.

"I *love* sailing," she pointed at his chest. He glanced down at his t-shirt.

"I'll get you one."

CHAPTER 2

*T*he Duck Dodge was utter mayhem, and Isobel couldn't remember the last time she'd had so much fun. Waiting for the start, boats veered every which way around each other. Tacks came so close together than her hands were soon sore—she wasn't in practice for this anymore.

After a particularly fast tack and back, Devlin tossed her a pair of fingerless bicycle gloves. She yanked them on gratefully.

His boat was so light and agile that the least breeze heeled them well over and sent them racing ahead with utterly brilliant acceleration.

By the time the starting horn sounded, he'd apparently used magic. Of the hundred sailboats, theirs was perfectly positioned, and they were one of the first across the line.

The entire nature of the race changed at that point. All the maneuvering and twisting for advantage fell away. With the bit in its teeth, the Dragon leapt forward with the rest of the fleet streaming behind.

Other than minor changes to the sheet as the vagaries of

the wind shifted around the surrounding hills, she could simply sit back and enjoy herself. They were third to a buoy that lay just before a low drawbridge at the northeast corner of the lake.

Coming about hard, they turned onto a broad reach with the sails swung well out to the side to capture the wind swooping in from the aft quarter.

In a companionable silence, they ran close by the broad lawn of the park at the north end of the lake. She could imagine ways to use it in the upcoming shoot. In the morning, the sun would catch the paved walkway that led to the top of the hill with a soft—

Isobel pushed that out of her thoughts. Tonight was only about sailing. The sun was off the lake and, though the breeze was cool, the air remained warm. It was so fresh and alive she wished she could bathe in it.

"Ever fly a chute, Belle?"

"A chute?"

"A spinnaker."

"I know what a chute is. I was questioning if you could fly one on this little lake."

"Hadn't planned on it, but that was before I acquired such a fine crew. Let's give it a try."

She shrugged her acceptance and he talked her through setting up the big spinnaker sail. In her experience, it was an awkward task of poles, lines, and a lightweight sail that wanted to twist and snarl at the least opportunity.

Except…not on this boat.

He'd made an utterly ingenious rig that included a small trap door at the very bow of the deck. She peeked below. The spinnaker was housed in a big cloth tube under the deck. It only took a minute or so to get everything set. They were ready by the time they hit the next turning mark.

"Ready about?"

"Ready as I'll ever be."

"That's the spirit. Helms alee." And he took the turn. Most of the way around he shouted out, "Now! Do it up, Belle."

She let go the jib halyard and hauled on the spinnaker's.

The big sail slithered out of the hatch and gave one loud snap as it caught the wind. It filled beautifully and in moments they were racing downwind. Instead of a simple white or color-striped sail like most spinnakers she'd seen, it was sewn as an elaborate multi-colored dragon flying gloriously aloft to lead them ahead at incredible speed.

Isobel could offer no answer to the sensation other than her laughter.

Devlin slipped close by the committee boat.

"Another one for your collection, my boy," Hank reached out a pole between their boats.

"Thanks, Hank." Devlin plucked his prize from the gripper at the end of the pole.

"You rafting up?" Sissy, one of Hank's daughters had her hand out, ready to take a line.

He usually did. The Duck Dodge traditionally ended with a whole line of boats rafted up to the committee boat. Dinner, drinks, jokes, and occasionally willing companions would drift back and forth across the tied-up boats for hours as night settled over the city.

But then he thought of Isobel. She'd be recognized in a heartbeat. In fact, he saw Sissy's eyes widen suddenly. She might be past fifty, Hank was in his eighties after all, but she looked to be on the verge of a complete fan-squeal meltdown.

He usually enjoyed hanging out, but—

He saw Isobel flinch, glance quickly at him, then slowly

work to paste on a pleasant smile that looked nothing like the one she'd worn throughout the race. She was clearly all too used to what happened next.

"Catch you next time, Hank. I'll bring some of my homebrew."

"It's a deal."

He waved and peeled off before Sissy recovered her ability to speak.

"Homebrew?" Isobel…nah, screw it. She wanted to be Belle; he'd let her be. Her voice was still tight, as she grabbed onto a subject change like a person overboard lunging for a life preserver. Afraid he'd recognize her and screw up the evening by becoming a fawning idiot.

"I brew a mean brown ale. Hank has a weak spot for it." He kept his eyes on the other boats still charging for the finish line as if she was of no new consequence. She deserved a bit of normalcy.

The lake was emptying slowly. Some race finishers were rafting up with Hank. Others were heading toward their slips.

He wasn't ready to go. Not because he had Isobel Manella aboard, but because he had Belle aboard and he just wanted to revel a bit more in how fun she was to sail with.

"You okay with puttering around a bit?"

"Completely," it sounded as if she was getting her voice back. Her shoulders eased as he drifted the Dragon all the way down to the south end, spilling air from the sails to slow their progress.

She seemed to enjoy the silence, so he gave it to her.

When he finally had to make a lazy tack to avoid running into the old Coast Guard lightship moored at the museum, she flipped the lines as if it was second nature.

"Damn but that's—" Then he bit down on his tongue. He knew better than to say the rest of that thought aloud.

"What?"

He figured silence was his best way out of this one.

"What?" But of course she wasn't going to let it go.

He shrugged in resignation, "A beautiful woman who can sail as well as you do. That's seriously sexy."

Rather than lacerating him for that, she arched a single perfect eyebrow.

"You're joking, right? Nobody says something like that in public any more."

With no better answer, he shrugged again.

"You're a strange man, Mr. Beast."

He laughed. He'd forgotten his role. "Roar."

"Doesn't sound like you're putting your heart into the role."

"I'll work on it."

She didn't speak again as the evening wind fell off until they were ghosting along the lake at only a few knots. Her face slowly faded into the night, except for odd moments when the city lights shone just enough to show her features. Quiet, peaceful, simply gliding through the night. There'd been no scene like this in her movie, where she simply enjoyed the serenity of sailing, but he loved that she felt it. Understood it.

The raft of boats slowly broke up, until the next time they passed that way, the lake was mostly theirs. The few craft remaining on the water were marked by their glittering red and green navigation lights to either side and a small white one to the stern. One by one, houseboat lights along the shore flickered out, though the city still shone bright beyond the south end of the lake.

A police boat slid by.

As much as he hated to do it, he figured it was time to send Belle back to her world.

When he eased up to the end of her dock, she stepped

lightly ashore without a word, then turned to face him. He hooked a hand over the end piling to hold the boat in place.

"I—" then her laugh trickled forth. "I was going to thank you, but I don't know your name."

"I'm The Beast," he added a growl that still sounded pretty lame.

"You're getting there. Keep practicing. Well, thank you, Mr. Beast, for the best evening I've had in a very, very long time."

He reached into his back pocket and, pulling out their race prize, he handed it over to her.

"What's this?"

"First prize in the Duck Dodge. A golden duck sticker."

"My! Such glory. But it's yours," she went to hand it back.

"Might already have a few in my collection. This one is yours, Belle. You absolutely deserve first prize."

"Why thank you, kind Beast."

"My pleasure, Miss Belle." And it really had been. Completely unexpectedly, she'd been more human and normal than any woman he'd been around in a long time.

"What's your Dragon boat's name? I feel that I should thank her too for the lovely sail."

He glanced down at the deck. She was *Unicorn*. Between being a Dragon-class boat, (myth liked myth after all) and having the single mast so tall and slender, it had seemed to fit. But—

Devlin looked back up at her, a lovely silhouette backed by the houseboat lights.

"You know, it's funny that you should ask that."

"Why?"

"Her name's the same as yours...*Belle*."

"No way," her bright laugh sealed the name change. The previous owner had named it for his brat of a kid, so Devlin had already changed it once ignoring the bad luck that was supposed to come with it. Maybe this time it would be a luckier change.

"Scout's honor." He'd been a lousy scout. Wasn't big on conforming to anyone's rules but his own.

"Well, thank you, *Belle*. And thank you." Then she leaned down and kissed him lightly. The smell of her was overwhelming. Cool evening and fresh air. Jesus, anything she brought to the screen was a tenth of what she brought to real life.

When she held the gold duck sticker to her heart with both her hands, he nodded lightly and gave himself a push off the dock. She stood and watched him go, but thankfully it was too dark for her to possibly see his boat's name, especially on the steeply sloping stern.

He'd planned on making it an early night, but he gave that up as the sails caught enough air to get him moving again. To sand out *Unicorn*, then letter and varnish *Belle* properly across the stern was going to take most of the night.

Worth it.

CHAPTER 3

*L*ast night, only Michelle had been waiting for her. Not exactly up, but in the armchair facing the entry door with a blanket tucked in about her.

This morning everyone wanted to know where Isobel had disappeared to.

"We thought the paparazzi must have chased you out of the city or something." Her brother would know she could take care of herself. They'd earned their Kung Fu black belts together long before he became a Delta Force operator, and now an ex-Delta operator and key member of Shadow Force.

"I was captured and swept away on a dragon."

Katie, the team's newest addition, asked carefully, "Dragons are still mythical, aren't they?"

"Ever day but Tuesday," she answered easily.

"Okay, I just wanted to be sure." Katie was newest to the team and the whole concept that there was such a thing as a psi talent was still throwing her. That she had one herself was still going to take her a while to adapt to.

Of them all, only Michelle was watching her strangely, but she didn't say a word in front of the others. Last night she'd been groggy enough that Isobel had been able to shoo her off to bed with few questions. But unlike her, Michelle was a morning person and was right on point now.

Michelle got her out on the back deck away from the others.

"What's up, roomie?" They'd been roommates for four years at Texas A&M, and a horrid nine months last year. Ricardo's final assignment for Delta Force had led to his torture and a long, long recovery in the hospital. They'd both been instrumental in saving his life. Living together through that endless waiting time as Ricardo healed had rebuilt all the bonds of college and more.

"What do you mean what's up?" Isobel was *not* going to be talking about last night. It was as if a small hole had opened in fame's reality and given her something perfect. She wasn't sharing that with anyone. Not even Michelle.

Michelle rolled her eyes. "Since when does the queen of practical, Isobel Manella, speak in fanciful language about mythical dragons. Was he really handsome?"

"Dangerously," Isobel answered with absolute honesty. She'd never thought to ask about his arm tattoos, but she expected they were something strange and powerful, just based on the bold lines and bright colors she'd been able to see.

And his eyes. Hidden first by sunglasses and then by the gathering darkness, she'd missed his eye color and was sorry for that. It made it harder to remember his face. The strong angles and warm coloring said at least partly Native American, but with a mix of a lot of other lines that had come together in a very pleasing form.

Michelle threw her arms around Isobel and gave her a crushing hug.

"What?" Isobel managed to gasp out.

"I'm just so happy for you I could cry!"

"What? No! No!" She tried to drag her way out of Michelle's embrace. But Michelle was five-ten of fierce redhead who was all arms and legs. Being just five-six made it hard to fight free without causing damage. So instead she went for Michelle's ticklish spot, third rib up on the right.

"Hey! Wait!" Michelle squealed satisfyingly. "Stop that! No! No! Aaaaaa!"

Even after Michelle had let go and retreated, batting frantically at Isobel's hands, she managed to find the spot again.

"Okay, I give. I give," Michelle raised her palms in resignation. "You didn't recently have fantastic sex with a dangerously handsome man."

"Thank you." Isobel felt she managed to pull her dignity back together reasonably well.

"Was it a dangerously pretty *woman* with a wild dragon tattoo?" Michelle whispered with one of her wild grins. Even as she spoke, she dodged back inside the houseboat.

A dragon tattoo. It wouldn't surprise her if that's what he wore.

Even thinking about it made her smile. He must really love his boat to have done that. She actually liked that about him, if that's what it was.

Then she turned to face the lake and there was every reminder a woman could need. The lake was glassy, and early morning traffic on the water was about workboats rather than sailboats. The whole scene was anchored by the tip of the dock sticking out just beyond where she now stood.

Last evening was a memory she was going to cherish for a long time.

But now it was time to get serious, and she started preparing herself mentally for the upcoming meeting.

It was strangely difficult.

Partly, it was that she felt as if she was returning all muddleheaded from a month-long vacation. Had it been so long since she'd taken even a few hours for herself? She seemed to have lost her balance.

And partly, this movie project had arrived from a completely unexpected angle.

Jennie Adams had used their old college connection to come to her for advice.

She'd written, directed, and filmed Isobel's first-ever movie. *Eve II* had been six-and-a-half minutes of Isobel sitting at a black table in a white room, having a one-sided argument with a perfect red apple set in the exact middle of the table...and losing. Jennie's school films had always been splendidly conceptual, and Isobel had starred in many of them.

Those days at Texas A&M were over a decade gone. Since then, Isobel's star had climbed until big-budget features were written specifically for her.

Her work with the Shadow Force: Psi team was real world and very engaging. But the movies were still her life. Yet even though she'd been finishing her prior film—yet another rom-com—two months ago, Isobel hadn't found any new script that piqued her interest.

Then Jennie had called.

She'd flown in to met Isobel on her last day of filming. The rom-com had been opposite the deliciously funny Hal Stevens, so it had been fun. But it was still just another rom-com.

She remembered Angelina Jolie's interview about the making of *Salt*. Producers came to her with a script for a Bond-girl role. She'd told them to come back when they were ready to give *her* the female Bond role. And they had.

But making that transition as a tall, athletic white woman known for edgy roles was one matter. As a short, curvy

Latina known for charming roles, it was proving much more difficult. She'd managed to have her character in last year's Western take on a Jesse James-level gunman role, but...

It felt like a cage.

Then Jennie had asked her to look over a script to recommend some people she might approach to finance it. She'd made a name for herself in small indie films and won several major festival awards. But this one was bigger.

In many ways, it was a classic Jennie script. She'd worked deeply thoughtful consideration of gender and race roles into an action-thriller.

The two hours Isobel had allotted to the meeting—mostly for old times' sake—had turned into three full days of talks. She'd even had the Shadow Force: Psi team help her do a table read. Not a one of them could act their way out of a paper bag, which had conveniently highlighted the script's rough spots.

Isobel could finance the whole budget for less than she'd banked on her last movie...if they were careful. Which was why her team had volunteered to come to Seattle with her.

For aerial photography, Jesse and Anton were Army helicopter pilots who had flown the team's Black Hawk helicopter up from San Antonio.

Ricardo and Hannah had been Delta Force operators and could cover *any* logistics or security issues better than a whole team of Rent-a-cops. She liked traveling with them because they somehow were exceptional at keeping back both fans and paparazzi without seeming to do anything. Another trick of the silent warriors.

Michelle was a licensed paramedic.

And Katie, with her wilderness tracker-trained eye for detail, was going to take on the continuity issues. She'd make sure that everything from clothing to fullness of a drinking glass was correct from one scene to the next, and that an eleven-shot weapon wasn't fired twelve times without filming its reload.

Isobel hadn't just taken on the lead role to save money; she *wanted* this role. The intelligent, modern action-heroine could be a new level of breakout for her career.

But Jennie needed help and, for the first time, Isobel had donned more than the actress hat. As the producer she was responsible for making sure everything worked. And Jennie had insisted that they be co-directors, which was both exciting and terrifying.

Isobel liked to lose herself in her roles, submerging fully into the character, and often remaining there for the entire shoot of the film. That was no longer going to be an option.

There was a knock on the front door.

"Time to gear up, Isobel," she whispered and pulled on her Ms. Practical persona.

Isobel took one last look out at the lake, wishing she could see a Dragon sailboat winging its way over the smooth water to come and whisk her away.

But she didn't, and headed inside.

~

Devlin surveyed the dock as Jennie knocked on the door of the lake's most luxurious houseboat.

How weird was it that fate had led him to this same dock twice in twelve hours? Nowhere near as weird as the one that had led Isobel Manella to step onto his sailboat last night.

Who had she been visiting here that had upset her so much? She'd sure been twisted up in knots something fierce. Struck him that someone needed his ass kicked for doing that to such a nice woman.

Of course she was probably a bitch in Hollywood: only

nice when it suited her. But damn she could sail. There was one lone fifty-foot ketch out for a breakfast sail. It's brilliant red sail ghosted along in the bright morning, much as he had late last night.

Maybe Manella was the Hollywood exception.

Yeah, he'd believe that when he saw it.

He'd worked on several of the big productions that hit Seattle and they'd all been the shits. And that wasn't counting the weird head games the actresses played. He'd bedded any number of them, wondering why they were even interested, until he figured out that was their form of slumming. Fucking a local was some twisted weird badge of privilege that came with being a Hollywood actress. Didn't have shit to do with wanting *him*, never mind any actual feeling.

If only the jobs hadn't paid so ridiculously well, he would have walked out on every one. But trading a month of his life for doing whatever the hell he wanted for six months wasn't a bad gig—once it was over anyway.

He'd tried turning down the actresses, but a rebuked actress was far more of a pain to deal with than a fucked one, so he'd rolled with it when they were in town. He'd certainly gotten to manhandle a whole lot of very fine bodies, even if there'd been no signs of heartbeat behind those perfect man-made breasts. They'd been the ultimate in no-strings sex.

He'd had enough. If this film was the same old thing, to hell with them *and* their money.

That's where he belonged. Out on the water before starting his day. Like an idiot, he'd turned down a perfectly decent welding job on a purse seiner out at Fisherman's Terminal for this.

He'd gotten the call for this little indie project that needed a location scout and local fixer. Jennie had approached him personally on Frank Morris' recommendation. The guy was a jerk as likely to stiff you for the bar bill as not, but he was a decent jerk by any Hollywood standard.

Jennie was an interesting one. So thin it was clear how often she forgot to eat. Her mouse-brown hair more collapsed than fell to the shoulders of her faded Texas A&M sweatshirt. And all she seemed able to talk about on the drive here was her film. Her fine fingers quivered with nervous energy as they poked and prodded the air to punctuate her thoughts. It was hard not to be drawn in by such passion.

He'd read the script she'd sent and was impressed. It had real potential, if no Hollywood idiot got their claws into it and dumbed it down. He knew the rule: There was nothing one writer could create that a team of twenty writers couldn't destroy. But there was solely her name on the front. Hard to believe it was going to stay that way, but it was a just an indie shoot, so maybe it would stick.

Jennie had already sketched in some settings, but he had a number of ideas there already.

"Dev?"

"Yeah, sorry, Jennie."

He turned from gazing at the spot on the dock where he'd left his Belle last night. *That* was the kind of scene they should have put in their damned movies, though it was too fictional to be believed. He sure as hell wouldn't if he hadn't been there.

His stomach churned up into a hard knot, Devlin followed her in through the big houseboat's door.

CHAPTER 4

"*J*ennie!" Isobel was glad that she'd suggested a breakfast meeting. She could feel her friend's ribs in their hug. Maybe she could distract her long enough to actually eat something.

"This is the location scout I told you about. Isobel Manella, Devlin Jones."

"Hello—" Isobel turned with her hand half-extended, then froze in place. "Mr. Jones," slipped out from practiced politeness.

Her nameless sailor. Her nameless *asshole* sailor who had absolutely recognized her. Who had let her babble on about sailing and being named Belle like she was some airheaded idiot.

He studied her face for just an instant, then his blue eyes went as stormy dark and dangerous as any villain's.

With a set jaw, he shook her hand as if it was a block of wood.

"Ms. Manella." Then he dropped it like he'd been burned.

She couldn't believe that he was going to play it that way. As if last night had never happened.

Fine.

Then so would she.

He didn't like that she was pissed? What the *hell* had he expected? Everyone was always trying to get a piece of her, and he was no goddamn different.

He wanted to be cold; he'd get cold. Besides, that's where her character started out in the movie, cold and calculating. She'd shift into the role now and save them all some time.

She turned her back and, unfortunately, faced the water just as a ketch twice the size of his Dragon slid closely by. How *dare* he take away the best memory she'd had in such a long time.

And the worst, the absolute worst, she'd fallen for it lock, stock, and "Cut! Stop action. That's a take!"

"Breakfast is ready," Jesse called them all to the table.

Throughout the meal, this Devlin Jones watched her closely. She, in turn, couldn't bear to look at him.

He didn't volunteer anything unless asked. Rarely offered more than one-word answers even then.

Closely? He watched her like some kind of bug. She was used to men's typical reaction to her, but not to the loathing so clear on his face.

She'd have fired him on the spot, except when he did speak, his suggestions were good. He clearly understood the challenges of angle and light—an essential skill for a location scout. An alley corner of a building could be shot in a dusky light for menace, while in dawn's first light, shot from the opposite angle, it could be an entry to a secret lab. A simple service door, set in the side of the same polished concrete wall and repainted appropriately could be a spaceship portal.

It also became clear that he knew Seattle intimately, as his suggestions sounded good, though she and Jennie would have to go see them.

Go to see them with *him*.

She wasn't sure she could trust herself around him.

How could the bastard dismiss last night as if it had never happened?

When he suggested they change a scene in order to set the bloody murder in the mayhem of the Duck Dodge, she'd had enough of him. As if he wanted to smear last night's memory with blood.

"How can you even suggest that?" She snapped it out sharply enough that several of the team around the table startled to look at her. She even heard Katie drop some of the dishes she'd been helping clear off the table.

"I can suggest it because it seemed like a good dynamic scene. You don't want to shoot it that way, no skin off my ass." His shrug was dismissive.

"I don't know, Isobel," Jennie's voice was soft as always. "I like the sound of it. The contrast of the underlying threat and the heroine's turbulent emotions versus setting does create a dynamic tension that we could play off Scene Forty-three." And she began flipping through her well-thumbed script.

"That's not why he's suggesting it."

Devlin shrugged again as if he didn't give a shit about anything.

He was suggesting it not because it was right. He was doing it to smear blood all over last night's memory as if he hadn't already ground his heel in it.

It was hard to do when her emotions were running high, but she forced open her empathic sense and reached out to him.

And *nothing* came back.

She could feel Jennie's sharp-blue focus. Oblivious to what was going on around her, she'd be thinking only of what shifts would be necessary to the script.

The rest of the team's feelings were clear. Confusion from

some, surprise from others, and a deep-seated worry from Michelle.

But from Mr. Devlin Utter-Asshole Jones, there was...nothing.

Nobody was nothing.

She could *always* feel someone else's emotions when she wanted to.

It was how she knew that Jennie hadn't changed a bit since school. She hadn't come seeking Isobel's help with this movie because of avarice now that Isobel was a success. Isobel could *feel* that Jennie had come for advice based on an old friendship built over hundreds of hours working together on student films. There were moments where she wasn't even sure Isobel's success had really registered on Jennie's psyche. She was just Isobel Manella from down the hall, which had been quite comforting.

But Devlin Jones? Nobody was simply a blank to her.

Unable to understand what was happening, she shoved back from the table and walked outside.

She could just hear Michelle announce softly behind her, "I guess we're taking a break."

Isobel turned the wrong way to escape and ended up once more at the end of her literal and metaphorical dock.

Footsteps landed on the dock, sending a slight ripple up its floating length.

She really didn't want to deal with Michelle right now, but she was trapped unless she jumped into the lake. A place she wouldn't mind if Devlin went. Maybe the Kraken would rise from the deep and eat him.

The footsteps stopped close behind her.

With a sigh, she turned to face her best friend.

Instead, Devlin Jones stood there with his arms crossed over a t-shirt that declared: *Sailing guy. Like a normal guy, just way cooler.*

"Like hell!" Isobel snapped at him.

～

"Bitch!" Exactly as Devlin had guessed. Actually way worse.

Instead of answering, she just folded her arms over that film-perfect chest of hers and scowled back with a snap of fire in those dark eyes.

Total bitch!

Christ, but wasn't that the truth. At first he'd stuck because he assumed it was all an act. Then he'd stuck because he felt some loyal need to protect Jennie Adams. The poor woman's script was going to get shredded by this…shrew. He didn't know why he cared.

Because he actually did? Didn't sound like him, but—

Oh shit! And he'd renamed his boat for her? How fucked up was that? He'd finished the last coat less than an hour ago, getting the flourish just right on the final E had taken far more attempts than he was willing to admit.

As soon as he was done here, he was going to go and sand last night's work right back off the stern. Maybe he'd rename her the *Stay the Hell Away From Me.*

"Look, lady. Do us all a goddamn favor and jump." He nodded toward the lake.

"You're such an asshole!"

"Me? What the fuck have I done?"

Instead of her scowl darkening even more, there was a flash of hurt. She covered it quickly, but he was sure of what he'd seen. Why the hell would she feel…

He scrubbed a hand over his face trying to scrape off the exhaustion and irritation.

If she…

"You think I planned all this?" Maybe that's what was going on.

"Didn't you?" She snapped back hard.

"No! Goddamn it, Ms. Bitch Manella. I didn't even know who you were when I pulled up last night. You just looked so damn sad."

"Oh, now you're the shining knight who rescues distressed maidens?"

He actually had to smile at the image. "Yeah, something like that. Arrived on a Dragon, didn't I?" Not a chance he'd be doing it ever again. That's for damn sure.

"I was fine."

"Didn't look it then, but whatever." He knew better than to tell a woman, especially a pissy one like this, what *her* emotions were. Aw, screw it.

But just as he turned to leave, he saw her crumble a bit. Saw the crack in the actress facade. He couldn't quite complete the turn. Not knowing what to do next, he just waited her out and watched the emotions cross over her face.

Anger, fury, confusion... Then back to a blazing anger that seemed born of pure Latina heat.

"Why did you pretend not to know me?"

"When? Last night? I didn't. Not until you were working the jib sheets. Then I remembered you in that movie."

"I meant this morning," her brow furrowed in confusion. "Why didn't you say something when you recognized me?"

"This morning? You're the one with the freeze-out 'Hello, Mr. Jones.' Where the fuck is that woman I sailed with last night? She was fun."

"Is that what you want? Fun."

"Better than this shitstorm any day of the week." And once again he felt the need to leave.

She took a deep breath and he could see a layer of calm sheet over her. Was that actress or human? No way to tell and why would he care anyway?

Not a chance of him plunging back into that confusion again so he waited her out. Again.

Just as she was opening her mouth, someone fired off a jet ski next door. She had to close her trap and wait until the nuisance had roared off onto the lake. Now if only this nuisance would do the same.

"Okay, let's start at the beginning," she said with a voice as warm as an Arctic wasteland.

"Don't do it."

"Excuse me?"

"Don't jump, lady. Whatever's wrong, it's not worth it."

She glared at him. "What are you talking about?"

"You said you wanted to start at the beginning. That's the first thing I said to you. Like a script, right?"

"Don't do it," she whispered to herself, then almost laughed. "Okay, from the beginning. Last night, why didn't you say anything when you recognized me?"

"Figured it wasn't what you needed. You've probably had a thousand guys hit on you, enough to make you damn sick of it. And also I can't begin to tell you how little use I have for ego-hyped Hollywood actresses."

She seemed to think about that for a while. "And this morning? What was with the black look and Ms. Manella crap?"

He held up both hands. "Hey, you can't lay that one on me, lady. You're the one who started it all off by calling me Mr. Jones, then looking at me like I was a goddamn bottom-feeder. Shit, woman, *you're* the one who kissed *me* last night."

At a loud squeak of delight off his starboard quarter, he turned to see that the back deck of the houseboat was filled with her people. All six. Only Jennie was missing, probably clutching her script and wondering where everyone else had gone.

"Sorry," the tall redhead mumbled through both hands

35

slapped over her mouth, but her eyes were dancing with delight.

He shrugged and turned back to Isobel.

She glared at her team before explaining, "I wasn't... expecting to see you this morning."

"Same. Same. But you're the one who turned it into a problem."

Isobel sighed and almost looked amused.

Damn but she had such an expressive face. In the bright daylight, it was even more of a pleasure to watch than in the soft evening light.

"Will you at least admit that you didn't exactly help things along?"

He matched her edge of a smile, "Only if you do first."

"Beast," her whisper was somewhere between a curse and a caress. It was soft enough to not carry to their eager audience.

He almost called her "bitch" in return, but thought better of it in time. Instead he'd rather remind her of the woman he'd met last night.

"Belle." He kept his voice just as soft.

Her expression said she hadn't missed the last-second shift but smiled at the change. Bitch or Belle, the jury was still out, but damn the woman was a stunner.

CHAPTER 5

"*H*e was the dragon," Michelle had followed her straight into the bathroom, and closed the door behind them.

Isobel flipped down the toilet lid and dropped onto it.

"He *is* so dangerously handsome," she practically crooned.

Isobel considered reminding Michelle that she was married to a former Delta Force warrior but decided it wasn't worth the effort.

"No, he wasn't the dragon."

"Then who was?"

"His sailboat."

Michelle's brow furrowed. "You know that you're not making a lot of sense, right?"

Isobel buried her face in her hands. She didn't need to use the bathroom; she'd just wanted a moment alone to unravel how she'd made such a mess of things this morning. And no matter what he said, Mr. Smug-and-Arrogant had played a plenty big hand in it.

Her gut still roiled as she thought through the morning's

fiasco. Fury mixed with nausea and she almost needed to get off the toilet so that she could barf in it.

"His sailboat?" Michelle sat down on the edge of the jacuzzi tub, close enough that only a toilet brush stood between them.

"I went sailing with him on his boat last night. It's a class of boat called a Dragon."

"How did you know him?"

"I didn't."

"You went sailing with a total stranger last night? Are you nuts?" Michelle's raised voice echoed off the hard tile.

Isobel didn't even know anymore. She'd felt safe and... free. It had been such a relief to just be herself for a few hours.

"You think I didn't check?" She tapped her heart because that's where she felt emotions when she did choose to use her talent. Perhaps it was placed there by a young girl's imagination, but the sensation had stuck.

Michelle knew the gesture and calmed down a bit. "Okay, so not nuts, just wildly incautious."

Isobel *had* checked his emotions last night.

And she'd *felt* him last night but couldn't today. In her experience that was impossible; no one could hide from her empathic gift. Yet Devlin had.

Or had he?

She had reached out to see if he felt avarice or lust.

And sensed...nothing.

Not just the lack of the negative or threatening emotions that she'd been checking for, but literally nothing.

Isobel felt a small shiver at the risk she'd taken by not being more careful.

"I can't feel him."

"Maybe he left."

Isobel shook her head. That wasn't the point, but she

didn't think so. Downstairs was still within her sensing range. She opened to the rest of the team and felt... curiosity. That wasn't definitive, but it would fit if he was still here.

Michelle's eyes glazed over for a moment as if she was concentrating on something else—a sure sign she was communicating telepathically with Ricardo—then shook her head.

"No, my hubby says he's still here. You really can't feel him?"

Isobel shook her head.

Michelle grabbed her arm. "Maybe he's one of the gifted like the rest of us. Has the ability to block emotions just like you can sense them." Her eyes glazed out again.

"What now?"

"I told Ricardo to not let him leave."

Isobel wasn't sure that was a good thing.

Devlin sat again beside Jennie. He knew that if he didn't do that, two things were going to happen.

Isobel's entourage—he hadn't bothered trying to remember their names—was going to start trying to take him apart, like a frog pinned to a high school dissection tray. And if they did, the second thing was going to happen: he was going to beat the shit out of a couple of them, walk out of here, and never come back.

Something else was obvious to him on Belle's side of the coin.

He couldn't miss the beeline that the redhead had made after her when Isobel left the room. These weren't just her sycophants like he'd seen so many other Hollywood types drag along in their wakes. They were her friends. And they were all set to smother the woman with their love and friendship until it drowned her.

He couldn't believe she was living with these people!

Christ, no wonder she'd been perched out at the end of the dock last night, willing to throw herself onto a stranger's sailboat.

They made him feel protective.

Well, that sure as shit wasn't any version of himself he recognized. No matter what Isobel said, the White Knight was a total miscasting. The best fit for him was the Black Knight, who took what a woman had to offer and didn't complain when she told him to get gone before the break of day.

Yet here he sat on his ass, working through the script with Jennie, while Isobel was being cornered by her "friends."

"'Scuse me for a moment, Jennie," he stopped her in mid-explanation of the hidden motivations of the male hero and how that was intended to play off an image she hadn't quite found yet.

Devlin breezed by her people. Two were back to cleaning the breakfast dishes and the other three were doing their best to appear nonchalant as they sat on a sofa and fat armchair. They were also sitting in seats with their backs to the view of the lake. *Dead giveaway that you're not ever so casual, dudes.* They were keeping an eye on *him* and he was getting pretty sick of that as well.

Devlin headed up the stairs. Open doors to four bedrooms and one bath.

A set of steps leading upward to the rooftop deck he'd seen these people lounging on last night.

No, that didn't feel right. The woman had been going somewhere to hide, not to expand. Up there she'd be seeking freedom, like on the sailboat. Right now…?

The master bedroom was easy to pick out by the big bed

and extra chairs. Houseboats, even monsters like this one, put a premium on space. This was definitely the master. The first closed door led to a closet that was entirely too orderly in his opinion, including last night's sundress.

Bingo!

Second closed door was probably the bathroom.

He knocked.

"Go away! We're busy." High voice of the redhead, not the sultry low-and-sexy of Isobel.

He shoved into the room.

Shit!

Isobel looked most of the way to miserable, redhead hovering close beside her.

He stepped in and went to close the door behind him, but it hit something hard.

Devlin turned to see the slender guy who shared Isobel's Latina coloring standing close behind him. Christ but the guy moved fast. And dead quiet. Devlin hadn't heard a thing.

"Bug off."

The guy simply eyed him.

He was a couple inches shorter. Devlin had done his time as a street kid and could see by the guy's stance that he was a skilled brawler, but it was still tempting to try. However getting Isobel's bathroom all bloody wasn't going to help anything.

He turned back to the redhead.

"You, too. Outta here."

"Go to hell, Mr. Sailboat Man."

He turned back to the guy behind him. "Are you gonna remove her or am I?"

The guy studied him for a long moment before gazing over his shoulder.

"No!" The redhead protested. "No!... I don't care what you—"

Like he was hearing only half an argument. Very weird.

Then she unleashed a lethal string of curses. Or they would be lethal if they weren't so mild. Apparently the woman didn't go much nastier than "Darn" no matter what her tone said.

She brushed by him, trying to land a hard shove as she passed.

Devlin saw it coming and braced himself, so all she achieved was pushing herself off him and crashing into the door jamb.

"Ow! Goddamn you!" She turned toe-to-toe with him. "You hurt her even a little and you're a dead man!" Then she stormed away.

The man watched him long enough to communicate that he'd deliver on the redhead's promise if she couldn't.

It was a language he understood. At his nod, the guy went.

Isobel still sat on the toilet, her long hair hanging forward over her bowed head.

"Some friends." Didn't need enemies with them around.

"Best friend and my brother. Married about six months ago."

"Yeesh." Kind of ties that he'd never had and never wanted. He'd had his run through the system and was long since done. His last set of foster parents had him over to dinner a couple times a year. Only decent ones he ever had, but that was plenty for both him and them.

"So what the hell are you doing here?"

"I'm certainly not being alone in the bathroom."

"Want me gone?"

She seemed to think about it for a minute, then shook her head and leaned back so that he could see her face. But she didn't speak, though she was staring at him hard enough.

"So, let's start with what the hell you're doing in Seattle."

Again that thoughtful study. "I'm trying to make a movie."

"With them?" He tipped his head toward the group downstairs.

She nodded.

"You sure?"

She matched his smile, "I'm sure. They're...special."

"If you say so." Wouldn't be his first choice, but what did he know? "The way I figure it, if you're going to do that, you're gonna need a hand."

"Is that an offer?"

He supposed it was. He held out a hand to make the point.

She took it and he pulled her to her feet.

Again so close that he could smell the glory of her.

"I suppose that I should warn you," she didn't step back.

Close enough he'd have tried dancing with her if it they weren't in a bathroom. Even on this houseboat it was about luxury, not wasted space.

"Ricardo, my brother, was a former Delta Force operator. And Hannah, the little blonde, was too. You probably want to avoid pissing them off."

Devlin had hung with his fair share of homeless vets around Seattle. Used be a whole cardboard box village of them under the Alaskan Way Viaduct before the elevated highway got replaced by a tunnel and was torn down. As they'd scattered, he'd lost track of a lot of good guys—royally fucked up, but still good. They hadn't exactly been the kind of guys with address forwarding.

While Devlin hadn't served, they'd still told him lots of stories, including a few about the silent super-warriors of Delta Force. A stupid part of him was sorry he hadn't tested himself against a genuine Delta. Most of him was sensible enough to think he'd probably just dodged a very embarrassing moment of being plastered to the floor at Isobel's feet.

CHAPTER 6

*I*sobel wasn't sure how Devlin had done it, but he'd somehow left all except one of the team back at the houseboat.

Her brother had put his foot down about her touring Seattle without security. And Devlin had made sure that security was Hannah, and just Hannah. Probably just as well, because if it had been Ricardo, Michelle would have found a way to come too, and Isobel wasn't up for that at the moment.

Rather than taking the team's Chevy Suburban with tinted windows, he'd fetched his own car. She'd expected a muscle car, which had been half right. She hadn't expected a perfectly cherry 1957 Chevy One-Fifty. It was dusky maroon except for the white on the upper rear quarter panels and trunk lid.

"I don't drive her often, but I figure most folks will be looking at the car, not the people in it."

"Which engine?"

He eyed her carefully.

"I had a 'boyfriend' in *Thunder Lane* who drove one of

these. I was a better driver than he was. The stunt team on the set liked that and they thought I was cute, so they gave me my first real taste of it. Couldn't get enough. I got the training and still do most of my own stunts."

"A dead man would think you were cute. It's the 283 with the dual four-barrel carbs." He made no comment about her skills. Either it didn't surprise him or he didn't believe her. Either way, she couldn't feel his reaction to tell.

"Race it much?" She kept the conversation going as she tried to find some way around his emotion block.

"You joking, lady? I've put way too many hours into rebuilding it to risk blowing an engine." But his smile said he'd run it a few times.

"Pansy." After holding the seat forward for Jennie and Hannah to climb in the back, she settled onto the luxurious bench seat. She'd forgotten the joy of not being confined by a modern bucket car seat.

His smile was absolutely a challenge. "Sometime when it's just the two of us, I'll bring out the '37 Bugatti roadster."

"How many cars do you have?" Isobel tried to remember the last time she'd been out anywhere as "just the two of us" and couldn't. Having her friends of Shadow Force: Psi slowly push aside the cluster of handlers that "protected" her from the world had been a relief. But last night had been the first time she'd done "just the two of us" in a long, long time. "Alone" was from some completely forgotten past.

"Only the two cars. Built them back up from mostly scrap metal and rust. Got an old pickup."

"Let me guess, a 1949 Chevy."

"I like the way you think, but no. It's a beater '95 Ford. Can haul around my boat or a new engine block without having to stress."

Isobel rubbed a hand over the rough fabric of the big seat as Devlin left behind the houseboat community and eased into Seattle's main traffic flow. She loved all of the room. The three-on-the-tree shifter left the sprawling footwell and front long bench seat open. It was just made for snuggling up close with someone at a drive-in movie. Not that she'd ever done that except while shooting *Thunder Lane*, but it was a nice image.

"Do they still have any drive-in movie theaters in Seattle?"

Devlin kept his eyes on the multi-lane mayhem as they circled south of the lake, but she could see his smile. "Did I mention that I like the way you think? Yeah, we've still got some. My favorite is across the ferry on the other side of Puget Sound."

That was the last time she'd been truly alone. Just standing on the upper deck of a Seattle ferry. Her breakout fame from *Where Dreams Sail* still ahead of her, she'd been able to leave the crew below and simply enjoy the sea air, unrecognized among a cluster of strangers.

"I'd like to do that again."

"It's a date."

She twisted to look at Devlin. She hadn't meant that, she'd meant be alone. And she certainly wasn't going on a date with a man she knew so little about.

Devlin must have noted her reaction. "Shit, woman. Not talking about marriage; talking about a ferry ride and movie."

"Maybe," Isobel could feel herself pulling back in caution. She again tried to feel what Devlin was thinking, and again felt nothing. This was getting very problematic.

She tried to figure out how to ask if he was aware of having any psi powers, without really asking, but wasn't coming up with much.

"Okay, I wanted you to see this tunnel first. It's brand-new and replaced the ancient Alaskan Way viaduct." The two-lane highway plunged down into a tunnel. "They dug it with one of those massive boring machines. We have two lanes southbound stacked over two more northbound. This would be hella tough to license for a chase scene or something, but it's a real unique Seattle fixture."

Isobel and Jennie had discussed the single car-chase scene. She wanted to keep it because she wanted to be the one to drive it, but the cost of a car chase had shocked her speechless. Underground ones were probably even worse.

She pulled the headset out of her purse and hooked it over her ears.

"What's that?"

"Headset camera. It's only video resolution, but it records what I see. That way I can review locations for the film later." She held up the small remote control and pressed record. "Smile! You're on *Candid Camera*."

His scowl was perfect.

She turned her attention out the window as the highway descended into the tunnel to dive beneath the city. She checked the feed on her phone. The image was clear. Tucked under her thick hair, there would be very little to see other than the tip of the lens as she recorded the tunnel's entrance.

"I doubt if the city would let you shut this down, but I might have a trick for you."

Isobel had never liked the sound of that on a film set; it was always someone who thought they were too slick, too smooth.

And typically it meant they were too dangerous.

Speaking of dangerous, just as they were exiting the tunnel at the far end, someone was walking along the narrow margin while two lanes of traffic raced by at sixty miles an hour. Even as they approached, he walked past the big steel door of an emergency pedestrian exit.

~

"What the hell's his problem?"

"He's an idiot?"

Devlin liked Isobel's snappy comeback, but that wasn't what he was referring to. The instant they were by him, he'd twisted around to stare at the car as if he'd impossibly spotted Isobel and was shocked to the core. Even now, his tiny figure in the rearview was standing stock-still and staring in their direction.

Christ it was weird. To be so famous that you needed to be moved around in the back of an armored car—inside a money bag. It sure hadn't looked as if the guy just had a thing for 1957 Chevys.

"So what's this 'trick'?" He could hear the distrust in her voice.

"It's called a rolling roadblock."

Isobel didn't react as Devlin negotiated them out of the tunnel through the heavy traffic, and got them turned around to head back into Pioneer Square.

"Make the run in the middle of the night because it doesn't matter underground. You get a line of cops running in front of you to make sure the tunnel's clear. Follow along with your camera gear and car chase. Then a line of safety cops behind you. Tunnel's only two lanes wide with no midpoint ramps, so four cops could do it. Wouldn't work if you were crashing or even banging cars, but you aren't. Run it fast and the tunnel will only be 'closed' for a couple minutes."

Isobel hummed thoughtfully to herself, then looked back over the seat at Jennie.

"That might work..." Jennie sounded less than convinced. A glimpse in the rearview showed that she'd plunged back into her script and was making notes. Which meant—

"Five gets you ten she finds a way to do that," he told Isobel. He didn't see any point in whispering as he doubted

Jennie could even hear him at the moment. "Of course, if the budget was really tight, you might try it in a single take. It would need some serious planning and a couple of good drivers, but it could work."

"Are you one of those?" Something about her accompanying laugh made him bristle.

"I know how to drive a car."

"Good for you. So does every joker out there."

"Rally school. Traded a guy a boat engine for a five-day course at his racing school. What about you?" He let his tone supply the "bitch."

"*Thunder Lane.* Stunt school. Remember?"

He did. It was just hard to attach those ideas to the shapely five-six woman sitting next to him. "Who's your third driver?"

Isobel hooked a thumb toward the little blonde in the back. Hannah was so quiet that Devlin kept forgetting she was there.

"What's your training?" He called back.

She just stared at him in the rearview.

"Delta Force. Right. Never mind."

The old heart of Seattle, dating back into the 1800s, was only moderately insane as it was still early for lunch. The parking gods smiled and he nailed a spot right at the base of James.

Across the street, Merchants Cafe had just opened and he walked them past the long wood bar and down the stairs into the old Underground Saloon. Every now and then Isobel stopped and did a slow turn with her camera to capture the setting. Gave him an excellent three-sixty view of Isobel in her flirty sundress—this time in softest lavender—with each turn.

Maybe, if the bitch stayed gone, he could actually enjoy this gig. The visuals were certainly exceptional.

Downstairs was all low-ceilinged, exposed brickwork dating back to Seattle's birth, a small bar, and cramped tables. His kind of dive.

After she'd done another slow spin, she popped the remote control in her pocket. No little red light, so she'd stopped recording.

"This is the other end of the spectrum, the new tunnel and the old underground. There used to be a whole level of the city here. Too close to sea level, muddy all the time, toilets that flushed backward during storm high tides, all sorts of issues. And I mean really muddy. Couple times they lost an entire horse and cart in a mudhole right in the street and had to sort of dredge for them smack in the middle of 1st Ave. They boosted the whole city up a story and just left this behind. There are a few leftover pieces like this open to the public, but there's a whole network that isn't. Underground tours can get to part of it. Tammy there at the bar could get us into the rest." He thumped his foot on the floor by the seat he'd chosen.

Isobel did one of her one eyebrow things at the hollow sound.

"Trap door into the old city."

Her smile said she was liking this game.

"There's probably fifty or more miles of tunnels under Seattle even though it's just three miles long and half that wide. There's a personnel evacuation tunnel that runs the full length of that new thing we just drove through that has some possibilities. Whole chunks of downtown, couple hundred buildings, are heated from a steam plant that's just across the street from here. Water mains almost as tall as Hannah weave all through the place." He winked at the little woman.

She offered back a deadpan expression and no words. In fact, he wasn't sure he'd heard her speak yet.

Tammy strolled over, far too chill to react to Isobel with

more than a nod. He ordered the Mac N Cheese with bacon and shrimp. He figured the three women would split appetizers or salads like they always did. On top of staying up all night to rename his boat, he'd been too pissed this morning to eat much breakfast and was starving. To his surprise, Isobel went for the Tuna Melt and a side of onion rings. Hannah and Jennie didn't slack either. By the look of her, he'd guess that Jennie only remembered to eat when food was put in front of her.

He refocused on Hannah. Isobel hadn't hesitated to point her out as someone capable of stunt driving. "You're really what Isobel said you were?"

Hannah studied him like a bug before finally nodding. Hard to believe, but maybe equally hard to argue with.

He turned back to Isobel. "You got any superpowers you want to be telling me about?"

Isobel didn't do one of her amused, raised-eyebrow things this time.

She flinched.

Before he could ask what that was about, Hannah twisted to face him. In that instant, there was a loud cracking of wood right under his butt as if his chair had shattered.

He lunged forward for balance so that he wouldn't be dropped to the floor. He ended up banging the table and knocking over an iced tea that would have spilled into Isobel's lap if Hannah hadn't pulled her instantly aside. Damn she was fast.

Tammy cleaned up the spill and replaced the tea. No problem.

He checked his chair carefully. Then the floor.

No sign of any broken wood. He sat back down carefully, not even a creak.

But the sound had been so clear.

Jennie at first, then Isobel began asking detailed questions about the look and atmosphere of Seattle's different tunnel systems. He'd found ways to prowl a lot of them as a kid, and was deep in answering her questions by the time the food arrived.

But he didn't miss Isobel briefly placing her hand over Hannah's and whispering a thank you. Seemed a bit heavy duty for rescuing her from a spill.

CHAPTER 7

By the day's end, Isobel felt as tired as Devlin looked.

After Merchants, they'd toured parts of the underground. Then they'd visited the steam plant, been given a look at some of their tunnels, and finally taken the underground light rail from Pioneer Square up to the University of Washington. There he'd talked his way into a new subway tunnel that was being bored further north and had definite possibilities as a setting, without having to interrupt any traffic flow or worry about other people.

Back on the surface streets, their progress had run into no end of problems and delays. All to do with fans wanting her autograph or a selfie with her.

"Your sundresses makes you too damn beautiful," Devlin had growled after she'd been accosted for the third time, or maybe the thirty-third.

He'd ducked into a souvenir store and come out moments later.

"Put this on." He shoved a crumpled-up t-shirt into her

hands. Snatching it back, he ripped off the price tag and shoved it back at her.

"I don't have pants and I have nowhere to change. We're standing in the middle of the street."

"Just pull the damn thing on over your dress. Gotta funk you up some, woman, or we'll never get rid of these fools."

"This is so not my color." Bright yellows made her skin look sallow and washed out. "And it will make my dress look ridiculous."

"That's the point. The great Isobel Manella would never be out in public looking less than perfect. Just put the damn thing on and don't give me any grief."

And she'd done so. Then she'd looked down to read it upside down.

Eat. Drink. SAIL. Repeat.

The "sail" was stretched to twice its already large size as it stretched over her breasts.

"You bought too small a size."

"No. I bought the perfect size," then he'd offered her the first lascivious grin since they'd met—though he made it a joke or she'd have hit him. Then he turned serious again. "Not a man born is gonna be looking at your face now. I mean, it sucks that you have to leverage that, but welcome to the warp in our society. At the moment my only other idea is a raincoat with a collar that zips up to the top of your head."

"It's not raining."

"My point."

And it had worked, especially after he yanked a bright blue (also not one of her colors) Seattle Mariner's ball cap out of his back pocket. With a quick grab and twist, he'd tucked her hair sloppily inside the hat and jammed it on her head. Then he yanked a tuft of it back out to hide the headset camera.

"There, now you look like any other sloppy-as-shit Seattle chick showing her anti-cultural-norms attitude."

"Chick" was one of those words that she really hated, but she didn't think complaining was going to help any.

Especially when he was proved to be absolutely right. No one recognized her after that. In fact, no one had bothered her for the rest of the day. There were still some who got past the ridiculous t-shirt. They'd look at her face with a puzzled expression for a moment, then dismiss the thought and hurry on. A few looked at her attire then looked away quickly as if she might try to ask them to sign a petition to free the lemurs at the Seattle Zoo or something if they made eye contact.

Isobel only made the mistake of looking at her reflection in a windowed storefront once. Utterly ridiculous.

But she was also anonymous. It was worth it—almost.

After they'd returned to town, Devlin had begun touring them through the city parks.

Volunteer Park had an Old World feel that didn't match the movie at all. Madison lost the urban feel, though it was an exceptional spot to sit on a bench eating ice cream and staring out at the amazing view across Lake Washington and up to the Cascade Mountains.

The more places they looked, the more they were able to cross off their shoot list. However, almost every one added to her list of places to while away a quiet afternoon.

She'd never had time to explore Seattle during the first movie. *Sail* had been her first major film and nerves had kept her perched and ready at the set even when she wasn't on call. Now maybe she could.

By the time Devlin dropped them off at the head of the houseboat dock, she felt as if she could barely move.

Jennie begged off coming in because she wanted to race back to her apartment and think about the new settings she'd never explored, despite living here for over five years as a screenwriter.

Devlin was proving to be an exceptional resource in several ways.

"What are you doing?" Hannah asked softly.

"What are you talking about?"

"This," she waved a hand in the direction of Devlin's car, now jouncing away down the waterfront lane. At the next corner, he took the turn and disappeared out of sight. Isobel hadn't been aware she was watching his departure.

"Shut up," Isobel teased her.

Hannah just shrugged.

Isobel looped her arm through Hannah's and they headed down the dock.

~

Devlin was hammered.

He hit the lounger on his back deck and collapsed into it. This was one of his favorite places to be. The University drawbridge buzzed with the sound of car tires crossing the metal grate. Twenty stories up, the I-5 overpass was offering a steady, low-roar of rush hour madness. He heard it as no more than as a counterpoint to what lay before him.

He rented the dock-level apartment of a three-story house that urbanization hadn't managed to drive into the water. In front of it were three slips to moor a boat bow-in. His Dragon was the smallest of the three, a sleek racer beside a bulky live-aboard sailing cruiser and a forty-footer Fat Cat showpiece that he'd never seen anybody actually sail in the three years he'd been here.

The view wasn't much, as this end of the lake was quite narrow, but any floating traffic between the massive Lake Washington and the ocean via Lake Union had to float right past his door. Everything from luxury yachts to NOAA research vessels floated past his back deck. He liked his slice of reality.

It was a quiet cloister. The tiny park just to the west was a real haven for ducks that spent a lot of time paddling around the three boats.

"Hell of a day," he told Broken Bill. The drake mallard had a broken edge to his yellow bill that curved up like a crazy one-side mustache. He and his lady had been regulars since Devlin had moved in with his Dragon.

Bill eyed him, but he'd forgotten to grab a slice of bread to tear up and toss into the water.

He held up empty hands. Hell, he hadn't even grabbed a beer.

Bill seemed to huff out a sigh before leading his family of three ducklings elsewhere.

Devlin let the rippling lake water soothe his eyes.

He hadn't much minded losing the night's sleep; he did it often enough when a project was going well, or even when a good book took him sideways.

But, good Christ, the woman was exhausting. The morning's emotional shitstorm had been the least of it.

Every second of the long day she'd been focused—without a single break. Across lunch she'd extracted every bit of detail his brain had ever held about the new Alaskan Way Tunnel and the old Seattle Underground. By the time they'd left the steam plant, he'd probably make money betting that she'd know how to run the place in a pinch. The manager had certainly enjoyed showing off his domain to a genuine Hollywood superstar with a brain.

In addition to being a seriously hot number, she was also an incredible actress. He supposed he shouldn't have been surprised that she also had a brain, though he was. It didn't take long to figure out that she was the smartest person in any room she entered. And she always seemed to know what someone was thinking before they did—simply fascinating to watch.

The construction and extent of the light rail tunnels had been next. What it took to drive a train, and to derail one, were gleaned from conductors and line managers who fell easily to her charms.

He'd always wanted to see the inside of one of the tunnel-boring machines, but it was Isobel Manella who'd extracted a promise to tour one later in the week.

The history of every park they'd visited wasn't enough, but also the types of people who used each one and what time of day.

She inhaled information.

It didn't just disappear there either. She did things with it.

He'd seen the front of the script, and only Jennie's name had been on it. But Isobel would suddenly turn to her and say something like, "That line on page sixty-three about the knife fight, what if the heroine's knife came from that display case in the Seattle Underground? I could smash it with my elbow or something. That would set up a real contrast with the modernity of her more familiar normal arsenal. Forcing her back into older patterns, facing older pieces of her past."

And Jennie would begin scribbling furiously.

The fact that they'd been walking through the Olympic Sculpture Park gardens at the opposite end of downtown, and it was six hours after they'd left the Underground, was irrelevant.

He'd also been drained after spending the whole day on some kind of hyper-alert. Constantly fearing for her safety. Sure, he was protective of any woman he was escorting, even the true flakes who really needed it. But he'd never been out and about with a truly major actress before, and that was unnerving all on its own.

Her own people were a real puzzle, too. Devlin had tried to keep it casual, but that Hannah unnerved him.

Not only did she seem to have eyes in the back of her head, but there was something else odd.

It was midafternoon by the time he'd noticed the pattern.

Someone would start to recognize Isobel—there was only so much a man could do with a t-shirt and ball cap to distract from that level of beauty. And just before he'd felt the need to intervene, the person would startle and look away.

By the time they looked back, Isobel would be well clear of them.

Eventually he noticed that each time they startled, he heard small sounds. Not very loud, but once he was listening for them, they were always there. A dropped pot, a bird call, a horn honk… Each one he could barely hear, but each was enough to completely distract the person. As if it was happening right next to their ear.

And finally, he spotted Hannah watching each one carefully until they were clear. Somehow she was tied to those sounds. Stupid idea that he did his best to dismiss.

Though it reminded him of…something.

He was too tired to come up with what.

The scent of seafood drifting over from the restaurant on the other side of the Montlake Cut earned him a stomach growl. Less that two hundred yards by water. He didn't want to get back in the car to drive around. And he sure as hell wasn't up for the most of a mile walk.

A sail.

Two minutes later, he was unlashing the last stern line. Not bothering with the engine, he hoisted the main and shoved the *Unicorn*...the *Belle* out into the channel. It was more than enough to ghost him across the channel.

But for some reason, he turned south into the lake.

CHAPTER 8

"We so need to put that in the movie," Michelle was mixing daquiris for everyone and serving them on the houseboat's back deck.

"What?" Isobel had shed the too-tight t-shirt, though she'd kept the ball cap to block the setting sun.

"That boat. It's lovely."

Isobel raised her gaze enough to squint out across the shining water. Her breath caught the moment she spotted it. "It's a Dragon."

Regrettably, Michelle wasn't stupid. She jolted upright, almost flipping a mango daquiri into Hannah's lap.

Isobel sighed. She really should learn when to keep her mouth shut.

"Swept you away on a dragon," Michelle repeated from this morning.

"He did."

"Mr. Kicked-me-out-of-the-bathroom Jones."

"That's him. And that," Isobel nodded toward the passing boat, "is his lovely boat."

For a moment she thought he was going to sail past

without even waving. Then she saw him gauging the turning radius to the end of the dock.

As he threw over the tiller to come about into the wind, Isobel rose to her feet. She hopped over the porch rail, landing lightly enough on the narrow dock that it bobbed but didn't try to pitch her over the side.

"Hey!" Michelle called out behind her.

Isobel reached the end of the dock just as the last of his speed bled off.

"How do you feel about fried fish?" Devlin's idea of a greeting.

"I'm from Texas," she stepped aboard with one foot, grabbed the rigging, and gave a kick off the dock with her back foot to turn him back into the wind before he lost all way. "We deep fry Froot Loops and chicken noodle soup."

"Together?"

"No. Though maybe someone has."

"Any good?"

She settled on a seat and shrugged. "I prefer the deep-fried shepherd's pie myself."

"Hey!" Michelle stood at the very end of the dock, poised to jump in and swim out to her.

Devlin let the boat fall off to catch more of the evening breeze. Even under just the mainsail, she moved beautifully.

"You're not invited," he called back over his shoulder. Then he glanced at Isobel, clearly asking if she was okay with that.

She resisted the urge to look over her shoulder. Instead, she opened up her feelings and sensed what lay behind her.

Michelle's helpless frustration. Anton, Jesse, and Ricardo were inside the houseboat somewhere. By their interest and general satisfaction, they were probably still looking over the pair of Red 8K movie cameras that had been delivered this afternoon.

Ricardo changed in an instant to sharp concern. Michelle had probably just called for his help telepathically.

Hannah was aware of events, and seemed quite neutral. She wasn't feeling any threat, but she'd also had the most opportunity to assess Devlin.

Interestingly, Katie's emotion was on the order of "You go, girl!" Seemed like good advice, so that was the one she chose to follow.

Isobel returned her attention to Devlin. "I'd never think to argue with the captain on his own boat."

"Someone trained you right, Belle."

"My mama done brought me up right proper, Captain Beast," she gave it all the twang she could muster.

"I dunno 'bout that. Deep-fried shepherd's pie, really?" His laugh was surprisingly soft. A warm chuckle that made her feel included rather than seventh wheel to her team of friends.

There was a proximity gone bad. As a team, they'd taken out a Mexican drug lord, rescued an ambassador from incarceration in the Congo, and stymied an attack on international undersea cables. As their latest mission into Indonesia had proven, the team had become a powerful, cohesive unit that could indeed find creative solutions not available to any ungifted group.

The problem was that they were also her circle of friends. There was no question that every last one of them saw her as Isobel, not as the Hollywood star. But they also saw her as fragile and in desperate need of protection from the outside world.

"Why do couples always think being single means there's something wrong with you?"

Again that chuckle, "Damned if I know, Belle, but they sure as hell do, don't they? Last buddy who tried to 'fix' me might have caught my fist with his face. Like tying himself down with a built, low-life bitch made him somehow better than he'd never really been."

"Then why were you friends?"

"Did I say friends? Buddy, which is a long way from friend. He was good with engines, at least until he started preaching from the holy-shit sanctity of the couple choir."

"You don't think much of marriage?" She tried to feel if he was serious or just yanking her chain, but there was nothing there to feel.

"Do you?" His face said he was serious.

She thought about her friends back on the houseboat. They weren't just couples; they were life partners. Even without the gifts that had brought them together, they made authentic couples. She'd felt their breathtaking connections at two weddings and an engagement party. There was no doubting the depth and truth of those emotions.

Devlin eased them up to a dock without her noticing. With the smoothness of long experience, he had the boat tied up and the sail down without her thinking to lift a finger.

What were the depth and truth of Devlin's emotions?

~

"They'll recognize me."

"Screw 'em!" Devlin had no problem taking someone down if they got obnoxious.

"I find that an acceptable approach," Isobel clambered out of the boat. Except she didn't clamber, she glided with a light step.

"You're trained."

"It's called being an actress."

He grabbed her wrist to inspect her hand for calluses, but she snapped it free with an easy twist. He caught the instinctive punch from her other fist, only inches from his solar plexus. Trained in more than acting.

"I'm sorry. You just surprised me," Isobel eased back.

He let go of her carefully. "Remind me to wake you from a safe distance."

"I've never taken down a man I was sleeping with."

Devlin really didn't need that image after a long day with her and went for the distraction of food.

"They've got nice sit-down service inside, or fish and chips out here on the barge." Ivar's dock was attached to an old barge covered with picnic tables. The restaurant and outdoor service sat on the shore across the gangway.

"Fish and chips."

"My kind of woman. They've also got fried clams, salmon—"

"Fish and chips. Chowder. Lemonade if they have it." She glanced around and pointed at the table in the corner that overlooked the water. "I'll be there."

"You be okay on your own?"

"I'm a big girl, Devlin. I can hold down a table on my own for a few minutes. Lots of people around." Yet, even as she crossed to the table, she was accosted for a selfie.

He was amused to notice that, despite the exhausting day, her smile appeared genuine for the photo.

By the time he was back with the tray of food, she'd reached the far corner of the barge and was staring distractedly down the lake. Her smile was different than the million-watters she'd flashed earlier. This was about her and her alone. It took her from Hollywood stunner to drop-dead beautiful. Gorgeous was too rough a word for such a look.

"Hey, Belle," he called softly to warn her of his approach.

"Hey, Beast." That happy smile didn't fade as he set down the tray and they began divvying out all the little paper trays and cups of food.

"Looking pretty damn pleased there, Belle."

"Do you know the last time I sat completely alone somewhere and just watched the sunset?"

"No," he burned his fingers on a piece of fish, but didn't really care as he dredged it in tartar sauce.

"Neither do I." Her tone was more wistful than sad. Isobel might have an angry temper, but sadness didn't seem to be high on her list of emotions.

"This was a gift. Thank you."

"Sure. By the way, you owe me twelve-fifty."

It earned him the laugh he'd been looking for. "It seems like I left my purse at home when a dragon swept me away."

"Seems like." He looked down at the boat floating below them. "I'll have to remember that she has superpowers."

"Of course she does. She's a dragon."

…and the memory came back. At Merchants Cafe he'd asked Isobel about her superpowers.

She'd flinched.

Then his chair had shattered.

No, it had *sounded* as if it had shattered. Completely distracting him from Isobel's reaction.

But his reaction hadn't surprised Hannah, giving her plenty of warning to pull Isobel clear of the spilled drink.

And all of those odd noises distracting passers-by throughout the afternoon.

"Hey," he aimed a French fry at Isobel. "What's up with that shit Hannah does?"

And Isobel's expression went perfectly neutral. "What shit?"

If he hadn't just spent the entire day with her, watching that face, he'd have thought she truly didn't understand. The casual tone, even mimicking his own cadence. The consummate actress had just slid into place. But because the woman he was getting to know wasn't there anymore, it was a massive red flag.

Devlin waved his French fry at her in a way to say he wasn't buying it for a second, then ate it.

"And I'm not buying that she had some weird audio broadcast device that I've never heard of, or you would have said that right away instead of going all actress-mask-blank on me."

She waited a moment longer, then sighed.

Now came the evasion.

CHAPTER 9

"I'm not used to having people be able to read me so well." And Isobel didn't like it. Her emotional shield had been built right along with her emotion-sensing ability. For survival. She'd practiced until she could layer any emotion on the outside, no matter what she was feeling inside. It was a very useful skill.

This time Devlin waved a chowder spoon at her in a circular motion to keep going.

"What do you feel—right now?" she asked.

"You're evading the topic."

"No, I'm asking seriously. What do you feel? Do you sense the people around you, and what they're feeling?"

His narrow-eyed squint said the answer was no. Which still left him a complete puzzle to her.

That meant she'd have to explain. And when she explained, his reaction was going to be all too predictable: disgust or horror.

"Can't we just leave it alone?"

He started to gesture again—

"Enough with the damn waving things at me."

"Ah, that fine Latina temper raises its hoary head once more from the depths."

"Go jump in a lake, Devlin Jones. Oh look, here's one right here. Go!"

"I'll give you three-to-two odds over the Kraken."

She gave him the finger.

He laughed, but set aside his spoon, folding his hands on the table like a contrite schoolboy, one with really powerful hands. Only surprise had let her twist her wrist free from his earlier grip. The casual power he'd used to block one of her better punches at his solar plexus had been…humbling. She'd always thought she could take care of herself.

"I take it that your answer is we can't just forget this."

He started to shake his head, caught himself with a quick smile, and spoke, "That would be a no."

"Have you ever met someone with special abilities?"

"Well, there was this girl back in high school who was so double-jointed that she—"

"Please don't finish that sentence."

"You asked," he began eating again.

"Damn it, Devlin, I don't want to spoil this. I was enjoying myself."

"Me, too. You're a very enjoyable woman to be around when you're not being pissy."

"When I'm not…" Isobel stopped before the words strangled her. "*You're* the one who's making me that way. You're just *trying* to make me crazy."

"What are you talking about?"

She waved her hand up and down between them like a mime feeling a wall. "I can't feel you."

"We aren't touching."

"Not what I mean. I mean that I can't feel your emotions."

"And you can feel others'?"

With no way out of it, she nodded. "Always."

"Huh," he took another bite of fish before responding. "So you can sense anyone's feelings?"

"Whenever I want to. Except for you."

"And Hannah can project sounds. What about the others?"

She could only stare at him.

"Pretty damned obvious once I spotted it. That Ricardo guy, your brother, arguing with the redhead in the bathroom. Never said a word out loud, but she was definitely going after him in some way I couldn't hear."

"They're telepathic. Only with each other." And she still couldn't read his reaction. It certainly wasn't any of the ones that she'd expected.

~

"The others?" Because it explained a whole lot of the dynamics Devlin had been seeing, if they were all gifted. He tried not to think of how impossible that was.

"Jesse is a sound amplifier for his wife. Hannah can only make little sounds."

"What? Together they can make sonic booms?"

Her steady stare stated that as fact.

"Shit! And the last two?" The big black guy and the cute English chick.

"He can see distant places without going there himself. She can feel where a person has been. Four are former military, one is a paramedic, and Katie is a highly-trained wilderness tracker."

"What about Jennie?"

"She's a friend from college."

Devlin liked that bit of loyalty. "What hold does that redhead have on you?"

"Michelle was my roommate all through college. It was

ten more years before she discovered her gift and saved my brother's life with it."

"Okay." He didn't have any brothers or sisters, but he'd bet that connection ran deep for someone like Isobel. He'd have to cut Michelle more slack in the future. Kind of explained why she was so protective of Isobel too.

"Okay?"

"What—you were expecting me to freak out?"

At her cautious nod, he could only smile.

"I've seen plenty of strange shit in this world. The way I figure it, until someone proves that there isn't a dragon flying around, why not? So you really can feel others' emotions? What's that like?"

"It's…like a window. I can see what someone's really like. Which has been very useful in my career. I avoided the whole casting couch creep show, because I could sense it long before it got that far."

"Show me."

"I'm not a circus act," she snarled just as nasty as a lion pissed at the guy with the chair. Hard to blame her.

Devlin shook his head. "Not asking you to be. You're just stretching my potential belief in the possibility of real dragons pretty far. If not for Hannah cracking my chair to distract me from asking about your superpowers, I'd probably have long since dismissed it, and you."

Isobel sighed again, but that sharp mind of hers didn't take long to reach the decision.

Even though he was watching her closely, he couldn't see any shift or change.

"There's a man behind me. Very guilty. Affair kind of guilt with lust and a need to hide mixed in. The woman with him is very pleased."

"Classic gold-digger type," he looked over her shoulder.

They weren't age split, guy seeking bimbette, but she was *very* well tended.

"She's also disappointed."

"To be eating fried fish out on a barge because he's afraid of being seen with her."

Isobel's shrug was expressive. "A young couple, somewhere off to my right. The fear is pretty high, but the anticipation is higher."

"Necking. Two women. Got their hands all over each other."

"They haven't had sex yet, but will tonight unless something goes wrong. Both young enough to be incredibly worried about it. Maybe it's their first time being 'out' with another woman. And yes, I knew they were women."

"That's a slick trick, Belle." He'd never have believed it if her descriptions hadn't been so perfect. And two women, two men, what did he care? The ones who shared his bed had breasts and no dangling paraphernalia between their legs. Someone had other choices? No skin off his back, though he'd never understood why a guy would want anything else than a woman.

"Slick maybe, but I can't read *you* at all. You could be a serial killer and I couldn't tell."

"Serial sailor, never happier than when I'm on a boat. Can't say as I much kill things outside the bug category." It was a relief that Isobel couldn't read him. Those teenagers definitely had the right idea. Right now, he was thinking about how he could get her the couple hundred feet across the cut to his place.

"What are you looking at over there?" She turned to look toward his place. Woman didn't miss much whether or not she could feel him.

He pointed. "See the two big sailboats in front of the

brown house? Third slip is mine. I have the dock-level apartment."

She studied him over the last of her chocolate chip cookie.

"The answer's no," he just wanted to be clear on that. Now that he'd had a moment to think about it, it was definitely no.

Isobel arched one of those eyebrows at him.

"I'm not interested in being the plaything for you doing a little slumming while you happen to be filming out of town." Which made him an idiot. She had the best body of any actress he would've ever been with. And he liked her, which would be an unusual bonus.

"I don't do slumming, Devlin. I choose *lovers*, and I don't do so often. So don't get your hopes up."

And why did he find that disappointing to more than just his libido?

"Yet," she dazzled him with that killer smile that was all her and no actress—then the damn woman stole half of his as yet untouched cookie.

CHAPTER 10

"You like him, don't you?" Michelle was the only one waiting for her, again. This time she was awake, sitting on the dock with her feet dangling in the water.

Devlin, being a wise man, had dropped Isobel off and departed with a wave but not a word. She tried to catch a glimpse of the boat's name, but the stern sloped steeply and there wasn't quite enough light to see. She still didn't quite believe him about the boat's name.

She sat on the dock beside Michelle, but only her toes reached the cool water. Again she envied her best friend for those mile-long legs.

"And you still can't read him?"

"No. But he's smart. He spotted Hannah running an auditory protection detail for me when I messed up."

"Weird."

"I know."

"No," Michelle wrapped a friendly arm around her waist. "It's weird for you to mess up. Me, I'm always putting my foot in it, but not you. What's up with that?"

She didn't know.

Shadow Force: Psi had been a thing for less than a year. And even now it was only just starting to find its feet. She'd certainly never set out to be the team's leader.

"How did I end up in charge of this motley crew anyway?"

"We had a secret vote. None of us wanted the job so we foisted it off on you."

At this point Isobel wouldn't be surprised.

"Man, you are in a weirdo headspace if you bought that line, Isobel. Of course you're in charge. Do you think one of us goofballs would have a cat's chance in a roomful of coyotes of pulling this off?"

"My brother—"

"Ricardo doesn't speak enough to be in charge of anything except a combat unit. I love him to death, but I wouldn't mind someone who spoke his thoughts at least on occasion. Thank God, he's incredible at demonstrating *how* he feels about me. He's really amazing in bed."

"I didn't need that image in my head."

"Well, he's awesome," Michelle wasn't to be turned aside. "How's Mr. Studly Dragon in the sack?"

"I wouldn't know."

"What the hell?" Michelle put her hand on Isobel's forehead as if checking for a temperature. "What were you doing all evening?"

"Eating fish and chips."

"Sister-in-law, your priorities are seriously messed up. You know that, right?"

Did she? Isobel's luck with lovers had never been high. Probably because she knew too much about what they were really feeling. Devlin's interest was clear—no matter what he said—but he wasn't making a big deal out of it either.

In fact, he'd turned her down before she'd even suggested the possibility. Which she *hadn't* been about to do.

When they'd finally left the Ivar's barge, a couple hours after they'd cleared away the meal, she was surprised that he didn't finally suggest heading across the cut rather than swinging her back down to the houseboat. Or, being Devlin, just take control and head that way until she said no.

Did she want to say no?

The lake had been so quiet and peaceful. She'd have loved to do another late night sail. But he hadn't offered. In case she turned his no into a yes?

Isobel lay back on the dock and stared up at the stars. Enough punched through the city lights that she could see where she was in the summer sky. Orion the warrior facing down Taurus the bull led her to her somewhat dimmer favorite, Cygnus the swan with Lyra the harp nearby. The dignified swan and the music fit for the gods.

So many nights she'd listened for that sweet music, but it had never seemed to find her.

And if she got any more morose or ridiculous, she'd turn this film over to someone else.

"Personally," Michelle still sat at the edge of the dock, "I think you should screw the crap out of him."

Isobel pulled one foot out of the water and tucked her knee up close enough to place it on the center of Michelle's back.

"Hey, that's cold."

She gave a hard shove.

Michelle's yelp of surprise would guarantee that she had no air when she surfaced.

But to protect herself, Isobel pushed to her feet and headed to bed.

Isobel checked in with her own feelings as Michelle sputtered and coughed before hauling herself up onto the dock.

Nope. No remorse at all.

~

Devlin was *not* going to lose another night's sleep over the woman.

The first had been changing his boat's name for her. What was up with that shit anyway? Stupid idea.

Yet, as he stared out at the *Belle* through his front window, she seemed to be sitting placidly, content with her new name.

He was so tired that he almost felt nauseous.

Closing his eyes only made it worse.

Lying down for five minutes felt like five hours and getting up wasn't any better.

A walk. Maybe some movement would clear the woman out of his head.

Devlin headed out the door, patted *Belle* on the tip of the bow, and strolled along the waterfront.

It was past ten, and while Eastlake still hummed with Seattle's traffic, three blocks down the hill, the silence wrapped around the small marinas tucked between clusters of houseboats. He liked this walk. When he was really in the mood, he'd walked the full six miles around the lake, grabbing a Chinese dinner at the halfway point. China Harbor had a dance floor that was always fun to watch over a beer. Sometimes even a little dancing and the occasional one-night tango between the sheets.

But tonight, his feet ground to a halt at the head of Isobel's dock.

Even as he turned down the dock, he knew it was stupid.

Sure enough, the place was pitch black. Everyone sacked out.

Maybe if he sat on the end of the dock he could *think* his way clear of her. Women *never* confused him. Amused him at times, but they were just their own people who didn't have all that much impact on his life. They'd come in, chart a parallel course for a while, maybe cling for a bit, then he'd drift on by.

But when he reached the end of the dock and looked back, he saw that there was a light in Isobel's room.

Devlin was tired enough to wonder if she knew the answer to why he couldn't sleep. Maybe, if she explained it, he'd be able to.

He couldn't knock without rousting her armada of friends. But it wasn't a big step from the end of the dock onto her back deck. Standing atop the opposite rail was all he needed to grab the edge of the master suite's railing and haul himself up.

Two loungers on the second-story deck, a cozy little space for two, but the door stymied him.

Ten feet to the right was another set of double sliding doors to another bedroom. So he still couldn't knock. The door itself was open to the cool night air, only the screen and an apricot-colored sheer barred his way.

He tested it.

Even the screen was unlocked.

Didn't this woman have any goddamn sense of survival?

He shoved it open and placed one foot inside, brushing the sheer out of his way.

That's when he felt a cold circle of steel press against his neck from behind. He'd bet it was exactly the size and shape of a gun barrel. It certainly felt as deadly as one. There hadn't been a single sound, which said either Ricardo or Hannah was on the verge of splattering his brains all over Isobel's bedroom—he'd bet on the former.

His eyes focused on Isobel. She was sitting up in her bed, the script spread across her knees, wearing one of those oversized t-shirts that seemed designed especially to be slid off a woman.

But rather than holding a pen and looking thoughtfully sexy, she was aiming a Taser at the center of his chest.

"Devlin." She lowered the weapon, but the cold circle of the gun pressed against the back of his neck didn't go away.

"Uh, hi." Okay, he usually delivered a better line than that, but he hadn't slept in two days and was definitely off his game. Having a gun pressed against the base of his skull wasn't exactly helping him concentrate.

"What are you doing here?" She didn't slip her weapon into a drawer on her nightstand, instead she slid it back under a crease in her pillow. *That* would be a good thing to keep in mind.

"I, uh, couldn't sleep."

"So, you decided that a little breaking and entering was the solution?"

"Okay, not my smoothest move. Could you at least tell your brother to holster his sidearm? I know it's him just by how chatty he's been about the way this whole scene is totally off-script."

Isobel glanced over his shoulder, then nodded.

The cold circle went away.

By the time Devlin dared turn around, the outside deck was empty and they were alone. "Jesus, he's spooky."

"My twin was that way since long before Delta Force got a hold of him. If I couldn't read emotions, I'd never have known what he was feeling while growing up."

"Okay if I come the rest of the way in?" He glanced along the upper deck again, but there was no sign Ricardo had ever been there.

"That depends on why you're here."

"Wasn't exactly sure myself. I went for a walk and seems I just ended up here."

"On the second floor of my houseboat."

Devlin shrugged. "It was on the way, Belle."

"I'd ask to where, but..." she tipped her head for a moment.

The cascade of her dark hair was utterly mesmerizing. It knocked what little wind he had keeping his mind functioning completely out of his sails.

"But," she came to some decision and smiled at him. "I get the feeling that I'm going to enjoy the answer."

The light flicked off. By the shimmers of the lights across the water, he could see the shadow of her sliding back down in that big bed. There was a flutter and thump as the script hit the floor.

"Could we lose the sidearm, too?"

There was a loud clunk of the Taser landing on the nightstand. Still in easy reach, but a definite improvement.

He checked once more that no one behind him was about to splatter his brains all over the walls.

Nope. Coast was clear.

He closed and locked the screen behind him.

He stopped at the edge of the bed and looked down at her dark hair spread over the light pillow. Too little light spilled into the room to see her expression.

"You sure, Belle?"

"If I wasn't, we'd be dialing 911 for the hole we'd just drilled in you. What were you thinking, Beast?"

He hadn't been thinking.

Devlin also decided that now wasn't the time to start, so he undressed and slid in beside her.

CHAPTER 11

"*I* love this camera," Katie was enthusing. "Michelle and I played with it for most of yesterday. It's amazing." She swung it up on her shoulder and aimed it at Isobel as she came down the steps.

Isobel was the last one downstairs, other than Devlin still passed out in her bed. What a glorious way to sleep. Lying on his hard, beautiful body after he'd melted her into a complete puddle of contentment. She'd listened to his heart and breathing until he was asleep, then slid just enough to the side that she could sleep wrapped around him. She'd woken in exactly the same heavenly position.

By the time she'd gotten out of the shower this morning, he'd rolled facedown onto her pillow. For the first time she'd seen the magnificent dragon tattoo spread across his shoulder blades. His t-shirt had revealed just the tip of a wing on one arm. On the other was the dragon's fiery head. It looked as sleek and fast as his sailboat, with its long tail appearing to be curled around his spine until it ended below his waist.

She'd felt voyeuristic taking the time to study it, and

finally pulled the sheet back over his otherwise unmarked body. It was some of the most beautiful work she'd ever seen.

Katie was still rhapsodizing about the camera. "It has so much excess resolution that we can mostly shoot a wide area. Then you can pan or zoom to partial-view but full-resolution images in the editing room." She peeked at her around the camera. "Do you always have to look so fabulous?"

Isobel laughed. Running shorts and the sailing t-shirt Devlin had bought her yesterday (it fit just fine without a sundress under it) was meant for him, as a good morning thank you when he finally woke up.

Then Katie blinked in surprise.

Isobel shook her head quickly before Katie could say anything. But her smile was huge.

As Isobel reached the base of the stairs, Ricardo glanced her way. She offered him a happy smile to show that it was all good. The smile back reminded her so of the quiet boy she'd helped raise while Mama worked—after all, she *was* twelve minutes older.

Then he shifted his glance in Michelle's direction where she was puttering about in the kitchen.

Isobel shook her head infinitesimally and Ricardo's slight nod said that he hadn't told Michelle, and what Isobel chose to do about that was fine with him.

She gave him a hard hug. Isobel had no need to open her senses to feel him, never had. The love there was deep and solid. The first message that had telepathically broken through to Michelle, as he was being tortured in some jungle hellhole, had been begging Michelle to tell his sister that he loved her. If the roles had been reversed, she'd probably have done the same.

She was still debating whether to announce Devlin's presence to everyone or relish the surprise when he strolled down the stairs looking as smug as the proverbial cat in the night. Isobel had always hated when men did that, but she expected that Devlin would be no different.

There was a knock on the front door. She was closest and answered it.

It was Devlin, standing there as if he'd just arrived. Though he wore the same clothes as last night and needed a shave.

"But—"

"Good morning. What's on the agenda for today?" *Then* came the smug smile.

He was giving her the choice of just greeting him or revealing that he was something more than that.

Isobel had never been one for playing games.

So, she pulled him down for a kiss right across the threshold. In seconds, he had her backed up against the jamb of the still open door.

～

Devlin leaned into that wonderful body of hers. He loved that she didn't spew any morning-after-denial actress shit. Sure, last night had been awesome, but he'd expected the cold-shoulder thing. Or flat-out denial.

He was surprised that she hadn't woken him and thrown him out before dawn. It was her bed and her prerogative. But instead he'd woken up with the sheet and light blanket tucked neatly around him.

Still, not sure about her reaction—especially after yesterday's fiasco—he'd decided it was better if she had the choice on how she wanted to play it. So, he'd slid across the outside deck and hopped down onto the dock rather than coming down the stairs.

But if she was game to greet him as lover in front of her

friends, and they didn't like it, he'd take them on, Delta Force or not.

He did take full advantage of the moment. Offering that awesome body of hers for a little early morning manhandling, he wasn't going to resist for a second.

When he heard Michelle's "What the fuck!", he figured that he was probably pushing his luck. He could feel Isobel's smile as she held the kiss a little longer with both arms around his neck.

Definitely his kind of woman. Yeah, it sucked that she'd be gone at the end of the film but, for once, he really was going to enjoy this shoot.

He did pat that fine ass one last time. Then he shooed her into the room and closed the front door behind him—eliciting a squeak of surprise from the other side.

Devlin opened it and let Jennie into the room before closing it again She must have been standing mere feet away, which almost made him blush—something he hadn't done since Marta Hegadus had taught him a few things behind the middle school gymnasium.

However, now it was time to face whatever shitstorm her crew of "friends" was going to throw.

Ricardo's careful nod didn't say whether he was happy or sorry about not having shot Devlin last night before he'd entered Isobel's bedroom.

The others were still too surprised to have any other reaction—except maybe he'd just slept with their goddess.

Except Michelle.

He thought better of her when the first thing she did was wrap Isobel in an intense hug.

Then she stepped up to face him. She was only a few inches below his six feet, except her Crayola red cowboy boots put them eye to eye.

"You hurt her this much, shithead," she pinched her

fingers together as if showing just how small she'd crush his balls given the chance, "and I won't need my husband to kill what's left of you."

She sounded actually serious, which showed just how much Michelle misjudged her best friend. If he hurt Isobel, Devlin knew he'd be lucky if she didn't shoot him herself.

He kissed Michelle on the cheek and whispered, "Dare you to try, Red."

Devlin had braced his gut in advance, so her fist just bounced off his abs.

"Don't *ever* call me that again."

"Whatever you say, Red."

His wasn't quite quick enough to avoid the boot heel that crashed down on his toes.

CHAPTER 12

"Let's review the video of the locations we toured yesterday. I think we've actually covered most of what we need." It had taken everything in her power to not laugh at Devlin as he'd hobbled about during the final breakfast preparations.

Jennie flapped her fresh-printed manuscript in a way that said she had everything the story needed.

Isobel could see that it already had a few marks on it, but way below the Jennie norm, so they must be close. She'd learned quickly enough on this project that Jennie-the-writer had lost none of her habit of near-infinite revisions in pursuit of perfection on the page. The surprise was how easy Jennie-the-director was to work with once she changed hats.

It was *possible* that they'd found the rest of what Jennie needed. Jennie had done a lot of scouting herself before Devlin came aboard. Isobel still had to see the Space Needle and the Opera House at Seattle Center, ride a ferryboat... There were a few others, but she couldn't seem to wrap her mind around much.

Devlin had made her brain atypically mushy on the

inside. To say he was a skilled lover was a waste of breath. Added to his hard, sailor's body, he was a natural-born recipe for success between the sheets—or up against the door jamb (her body was still buzzing from that good-morning kiss). But there hadn't been a single instant where she had the impression he was making love to the international film star. When it was just them, she was the staunch Belle to his playful Beast. Again, no way to tell for certain, but it had definitely felt that way.

Isobel ordered herself to focus.

Everyone was gathered in the living room end of the houseboat's main floor. It was a surprisingly flexible space that was working well for the start of the film. People were nursing their second cups of coffee as they sat in the chairs and sofas facing the big screen TV.

"This is the footage I captured yesterday."

Hannah began running the playback from Isobel's headset video camera.

The first flash on the screen was Devlin's eye roll as she announced he was on *Candid Camera.*

"Hey," Michelle piped up. "The camera really likes this dingbat."

Isobel looked at it critically. It was true. There were some people that a movie camera simply...liked. There were also ones it hated, making wide-set eyes look manic or adding way more than an apparent ten pounds. Devlin's dark good looks and clear features made him particularly attractive on screen. She looked to the man himself. He was damned attractive in life, too. And he knew it. He didn't flaunt it in any way, looking more the rough-and-ready type, but it was there.

He must have noticed her attention, "Not a chance in hell."

She was almost tempted to cast him in a small cameo just to tease him, but Jennie was suddenly very talkative.

"I think we can use this tunnel twice. Once in the opening, setting the tension as Isobel proceeds south at the start of the case, unaware that she's already being followed—page eleven. Again, but going in the other direction for the page eighty-four car chase. It would start inside the steam plant, jump to the cars, and then up the reverse tunnel, which ends near the Opera House for the final scene. It could be very dramatic."

"Now all we have to do is fill in from page eleven to eighty-four," Devlin quipped.

Jennie flapped her manuscript at him and turned back to the screen.

Isobel thought about it. The north and southbound lanes were actually stacked in a fifty-six-foot concrete tube bored under the city. The southbound lanes were on top, so there was less of a descent to enter the tunnel.

The northbound lanes, that would appear later in the manuscript, descended deeper, to travel below the southbound ones.

"I like the metaphor." All she had to do was indicate the varying depths with her hands for Jennie to get it. Her rapid paging through the screenplay caused Devlin to laugh. It was as if he welcomed Jennie's odd ways rather than merely tolerating them.

Was that how he felt about her, pleased by her *not* being part of the human norm? It had always made her the outsider, the one who didn't belong. But she'd never considered embracing it. Instead, she'd done her best to hide her differences and conform.

She flipped the question around. Was it pleasing that she *couldn't* read him? Perhaps.

If that—

"What a goon," Michelle was looking at the screen. They were passing the man who had walked along the high-speed traffic lane inside the tunnel. No reflective vest or other warning gear. He strode along in a black t-shirt, jeans, and heavy boots.

Isobel barely remembered him.

"He had a serious case of something," Devlin observed. "He spun around to watch us pass as if we'd thrown food at him while going sixty. I can't imagine he recognized Isobel. The daylight at the end of the tunnel would have been reflecting off the windshield at that point."

"It wasn't interest," Hannah said softly. "I turned and caught a glimpse of him face-to-face through the rear window." She trailed off and wrapped her arms together as if she was cold.

"What in Sam Hill does he have against beautiful women?"

"It was..." but she couldn't seem to complete the sentence.

"Was what, hon?" Jesse draped an arm across her shoulders.

She leaned into him briefly, a gesture Isobel had only seen her make a few times. Hannah wasn't much for leaning on anyone, not even the man she loved and had married.

Isobel opened up and felt that Hannah wasn't feeling thoughtful, she was unnerved—jagged black spikes overlaying her Kelly-green reliability. What did it take to unnerve a Delta operator?

"I don't know how to explain it." Rather than turning to Jesse, she turned to Ricardo. "You've seen it. Like religious mania but on the battlefield."

Ricardo grunted as he chewed on that for a moment. Everyone knew to give him a bit of time to find his words.

Devlin started to speak, but stopped at Isobel's headshake. Ricardo took Michelle's hand and began toying with it.

She must have asked him a question telepathically because he nodded before speaking.

"The jihadis and the religious crusaders called it 'Battle Ecstasy.' Those who faced the Vikings, the Celts or Scots, and others called it 'Battle Frenzy.' I think that the Irish legends came closer, calling it the 'Battle Fury.' Had a unit commander who called them 'Glory Killers.' The ones who live for the joy of battle and wielding death. Never had much truck with that type."

Hannah shivered and Isobel realized that she herself was rubbing her arms against goosebumps.

"One screwed-up soul. Glad we don't have any of those in this movie," Devlin shrugged breaking the mood. "We don't, do we, Jennie?"

She actually flipped to the cast list at the front and scanned it. "No. No frenzied warriors." Then she must have heard herself. She made a show of looking over the scene summary as well. "And no maniacal battles. Unless you'd like to star in one, Devlin?"

"Not me. That *Candid Camera* scene was more film that I ever wanted," but then he did turn serious, serious and a little sad. "Met enough guys like him out there on the streets. Maybe not that kinda messed up, but way out there. Feel sorry for whatever poor bastard ends up in his sights. Guy must hate the world or something."

Isobel didn't want to think about any of that, and restarted the video to lead the others through what else they'd seen yesterday.

They ended going through it several times, even penciling in primary camera angles on the shot sheet for several of them.

Jennie had always favored continuous takes for impact.

And Isobel was a fan of one-take filming.

The combination was hard on the actresses and the crew.

95

Despite that, the actress in her liked the freshness, the aliveness that it brought to the performance. Knowing there was only the one take, the energy was high and the pressure would translate well to the genre.

And since she'd underwritten the film, the businesswoman in her liked the savings of minimizing expensive resets and retakes.

But each time through the video she'd shot, she had to look away from the man at the end of the tunnel.

~

During lunch break, Devlin was sitting alone on the back deck. He didn't want to make assumptions or get in the way.

Yeah, load of crap.

He wanted to get his hands back on Isobel so badly that the only safe answer was distance. Distance and—

"Who the fuck *are* you?" Michelle dropped a plate in his lap with a monster egg salad sandwich on a Kaiser roll and a large bag of vinegar and sea salt Kettle chips. She made a show of shaking the can of Coke hard before tossing it to him.

Then she dropped into the chair next to him with the same lunch, except he'd assume her can was unshaken, and crossed her red boots.

"Thanks, Red," he set the unopened Coke aside carefully and bit into the sandwich. "Devlin Jones. Part-time movie fixer, do a little boat building, some specialty welding, whatever comes to hand."

"And Isobel just 'came to hand'?"

"A) Question for Isobel. B) None of your goddamn business as far as I'm concerned. And C) Do you enjoy being such a redheaded-temper-tantrum cliché, Red, or are you doing this special for me?" He looked up from his sandwich when she didn't answer.

She finally muttered a soft, "Crumbs."

"What?"

"I hate, really, really *hate* that you're right."

"Way I see it, Red, you're just trying to protect your best friend. Gets you a lot of points in my book. Except I don't see Isobel as the kind of woman who needs a lot of protection. Could probably do with a little less of it from all of you."

"You don't get it, jerk," she'd apparently decided she was enjoying her temper. "Isobel Manella is special, seriously special."

"Might have figured that out for myself," he opened up the bag of chips and layered some into his sandwich. The salt-vinegar-crunch was a nice addition.

"No, I mean—" And she huffed in frustration. Two would get him ten she was fighting for some way to be discreet.

Devlin considered letting her dangle, but he was getting to like her fire and loyalty. "Look, Red, why don't you ask your husband what he thinks about all this? I'll wait. Go ahead, ask him." He reached out and flicked a finger against her temple.

Her eyes shot wide as she stared at him with her jaw flapping in the wind.

"Welcome to the game, Red."

"I wish you'd stop calling me that," she recovered enough to take a first vicious bite out of her own sandwich.

"Would've long ago if it didn't piss you off so much."

She chewed on that one and her sandwich for a while, before offering him a smile. "Could get to like you, Mr. Devlin Jones."

"Mutual, Red."

"Then again, maybe not."

CHAPTER 13

*W*aiting.
Just waiting.

His government, the US government, had taught him well. They'd trained him, steeped him, in the power of waiting.

It wasn't the waiting that was hard, it was the patience. It gnawed at him like the wolf who'd almost taken him out on the Mirny, Siberia, mission. It had been a silent battle to the death less than fifty meters from a fully armed Russian patrol. But they'd trained him well, and he'd returned with proof of the deadly poisons that the FSB created in that closed city, and a permanent limp.

They'd taught him waiting again when he'd gone from loyal subject to lab rat. When they'd burned his gift out of him, scraped it clean with chemicals meant to enhance it, reproduce it. And when it was gone, and they'd discarded him into a deep and dark cell, he had waited.

Three years he'd been caged in the dark before opportunity had shone her smile upon him. He'd left a dozen scientists and guards buried in a fifty-meter crater in the Nevada desert. He alone had walked out, walked across that vast burning desert undetected. His government had taught him well.

He'd disappeared into the warp and fold of civilians, unknown, unremarked.

Knowing it was all gone, that his gift would never return, he had merely existed.

Until he'd felt...her!

He no longer had the gift, but he'd felt it in her like a beacon of wildfire. All he could feel was that she had everything he'd lost.

A signal that he knew would let the evil ones track her, lock her into a lab, and dissect her soul until only a screaming shell remained.

No, it was better if she was saved now. Never knew that dark hole underneath the shifting soils of the Nevada desert.

His government had taught him that the only easy day was yesterday.

They'd taught him that lesson very, very well.

He waited.

CHAPTER 14

$\mathcal{R}$ather than waiting for the full crew to arrive, Isobel decided to start shooting some of the simpler scenes. Everything the team could do themselves saved money.

As they were shooting the script in order, mostly, that meant that she would start driving from the top of Queen Anne Hill, descending into the city, running past the Opera House—with no other hint that the climax and aftermath would happen there—and then weave over to the southbound tunnel.

No need for any permits or police escorts for that drive as they weren't going to be speeding, stopping unexpectedly, or breaking any other traffic laws. She didn't even have to run any lines, because the opening sequence was all internal dialog and all shot from behind as a roll under the opening credits.

Isobel would record that audio during the edit.

She slid into the seat of Devlin's beautiful Chevy just as dawn etched the sky.

"Don't you be dinging up my, baby, you hear?" Devlin

rubbed a loving hand over the fender. After a second night together, she knew the touch of those roughly strong hands. Would it bother a man like him if she pointed out what a tender lover he was? Tender yet wonderfully teasing? Probably.

She'd have smiled at him, but that wasn't her character and she was now Rosamarie Cruz.

"Hear you. I still can't believe you're letting me drive this." She'd never felt better or more ready to start shooting a scene.

Without asking, Jennie had simply incorporated his car into the script. They'd originally talked about a Columbo-style beater, but hadn't settled on anything. Instead of the scheduled trip to the crappy used car lots that Devlin had assured her were strung for miles along Aurora Ave, she was now sitting at the helm of his '57 Chevy.

She imagined the heat of his hands on the thin wheel, her fingers overlapping his.

Yes, she'd have to pursue that idea the next time they were in bed together. Their first night had been about satisfying sexual urges, and sleep. The second had been pure fun. She was looking forward to what more there was for them.

The movie! She ordered herself for the tenth—or so—time since waking curled up in his arms.

Part of her character was being an ace mechanic. Former military motor pool, so Rosamarie had skills. Recently former, so she had no new path yet in the confusion of the civilian world. That's why Isobel had spent long hours with the ex-military of her team, trying to get her head inside that shift.

That's what had been missing from Jennie's script. She'd had the story—at its heart, a tale of disenfranchisement from one form of a life to another. But not the detail of emotion that Ricardo, Hannah, and the others had and, much to her surprise, were still going through.

The meta-layer of her own life's transition from strictly being an actress over to producer and co-director was not lost on her.

By the end of the movie... Maybe by then she'd have some clue of what her own future should look like.

For now she'd focus on the film's beginning.

Michelle sat in the back seat with one of the Red 8K cameras. It would capture her from behind for the whole drive so that the audience felt as if they were along for the ride.

Hannah, Devlin, Ricardo, and Katie were in a rented Jeep Wrangler. Hannah drove. In the back, Ricardo was handling communications, and she supposed that Devlin was along to make sure she didn't ding his car. They'd folded back the top and pushed the front windshield down so that Katie had an unimpeded view with the camera from the passenger seat.

Anton and Jesse were up in the team's Black Hawk. It already had a hi-res camera built into the surveillance package. Timing was going to be everything here.

The Black Hawk couldn't linger over downtown Seattle airspace. So, when it started its overflight, they had to be ready and on the move. Over Queen Anne, it could delay in the narrow slot between minimum ground clearance below and the air traffic control area above for the approaches to two major airports. Once they headed for the tunnels, the helicopter was going to be responding to air traffic controllers for a landing at Boeing Field. It could follow her drive only once, then it was done.

"Ricardo said the helo is ready to start its run," Michelle spoke from the back seat.

"Rolling?"

"Rolling," Michelle confirmed.

Isobel started the car. They pulled out of the Queen Anne hill parking lot; the condos had once been a high school building and looked it. No location shots planned inside, so all they'd done was hang out in the parking lot for a bit. Devlin had suggested it for the sweeping view of the city's high rises and highway swoops. The metaphor of her plunging down into its morass had appealed to Jennie.

The light was perfect. It would start golden, but be stark-reality bright by the end of the drive into downtown.

She loved the feel of the Chevy's big engine. It wasn't all graceful and quiet like modern engines. You *knew* it was cranking over, making the car shudder as if anticipating a release.

"Not on this run, baby," she patted the dashboard.

"Good, nice human touch," Michelle announced from the back seat behind her camera.

Isobel resisted the urge to glare at her as she turned onto the main street and descended the cliff-steep front of Queen Anne Hill down into an old-town commercial district thick with cars. The Chevy's first gear wound up the engine's rpm until it was almost a fever pitch. They'd probably have to tone that down in the final mix or it would be too much too soon.

The base of the hill was a locals' area, too far from the main core of the city to be a tourist haven. In three blocks she spotted at least ten restaurants she wanted to try: Italian, breakfast hole-in-the-wall, Mexican—it looked amazing.

She'd memorized the turns, but Ricardo fed them to her through Michelle anyway.

A left turn took her along the north edge of Seattle Center. A playhouse, the ballet, and the Opera House all slid by on her right. Here was the film's ending.

In the following Jeep, Katie knew to make sure she had a clear pan of its modernist frontage and the high-hung wire nets on which nighttime colors and patterns could be projected.

Getting the opera's cooperation had been easy, half of their income came from donations, not tickets. Isobel had simply offered them a six-digit donation—she liked supporting the arts anyway. After that, she could have blown up the Opera House and they might not have complained.

A few blocks up, she turned right and merged onto southbound Route 99. Just before it plunged into the tunnel, she wanted to check on the helicopter overhead, but that would be a break of character. On the sly, she checked that the Jeep Wrangler was still in position.

No!

That was Isobel.

She was now Rosamarie. Perhaps her emergence from the buffered cocoon of the military would have her being paranoid and checking behind her—clearing her six—more suspiciously. She made a point of it, not even noticing the Jeep and her teammates riding along anymore. She was now Rosamarie Cruz and didn't trust anyone or anything.

She was an ex-military, ace mechanic, heading south through Seattle to a job interview. A job interview that was going to go terribly wrong.

Then she plunged into the tunnel's darkness.

≈

"He's in a hurry."

Devlin glanced forward to see Hannah checking the rearview mirror.

He twisted around to see what she was looking at.

Coming fast out of a parking lot, a bright yellow Hummer did a four-wheel drift onto the ramp and was approaching fast behind them.

"Don't let him screw up my shot," Katie called out, but didn't look away from her camera's viewscreen. She wore a Steadicam rig that let the camera float smoothly despite any bumps in the road and most jostles by the operator.

"May not have a choice. He's coming hard." Devlin tried to see the driver, but they'd descended into the leading edge of the tunnel and all he saw were the strobed reflections of the overhead lights bouncing off the windshield.

The roar of the Hummer's engine quickly overwhelmed the heavy thud that the '57 Chevy was leaving in its wake.

"He's not changing lanes. Sorry, Katie, just try to keep it smooth." Then Hannah shifted over to the left lane.

The Hummer followed them.

"Okay, that's not a good sign." There'd been no reason for the Hummer to have followed them.

Devlin glanced ahead. Isobel was still cruising along in her lane. They were deep in the tunnel now. Rare for Seattle and its traffic issues, the steady flow of cars was well-spaced and cruising at highway speeds. There'd been no reason for the Hummer to have followed them.

It felt surreal, like being under full sail just before a storm crashed down and shredded your sails because you'd left them up too long.

Hannah switched back, and so did the Hummer.

He started calling out distances, "Five car lengths, four, three—do some of that amazing driver shit, Hannah—two—"

At one, she jolted into the other lane and slammed on the brakes.

Devlin was nearly gutted by the seatbelt as the Jeep tried to stand on its nose.

The Hummer blew by just inches away, swerving at them but missing.

"Do you think he doesn't like Jeeps?" Ricardo offered one of his rare dry comments.

"It's him." Devlin had seen his face. The Hummer had a new car sticker still on the rear window.

"Him who?"

"Warn Isobel," the Hummer was already accelerating toward her in the Chevy. "It's the guy from the tunnel. This tunnel. He's been waiting for her. Warn her!" He shouted the last at Ricardo.

Who did nothing except gaze into the distance.

"Why aren't you warning her?" Devlin grabbed Ricardo's arm and shook him.

Ricardo reached over casually, pinched some nerve on Devlin's arm that hurt like fucking wildfire. He casually released it, and Devlin snatched his arm back.

"I already did warn her. Through Michelle."

Devlin had to shake himself. It was one thing knowing about it. It was another thing watching telepathy in action. If he—

Isobel was accelerating hard, but the Hummer was a massively overpowered vehicle, and sixty years' of technology newer.

It leapt after her.

Hannah was chasing in the Jeep, but there was no chance of overtaking the Hummer in time. Or of Isobel pulling ahead.

"Where's the bottle?" Ricardo asked in that deadpan tone of his.

It steadied Devlin's nerves just enough for him to think.

The bottle?

Why was Ricardo asking—

He wasn't!

Michelle was.

For Isobel.

The bottle of nitrous oxide. Boost juice! The drag racer's best friend.

"Under the seat, valve by her right foot. The arming switch is under the dash above her right knee. Then put her foot down—hard!" Devlin was having trouble breathing.

The Hummer was almost in striking range, and it wasn't slowing down.

"Three, two..." Hannah was counting.

On one, just moments before the Hummer slammed into the Chevy's tailfins, the old 150 leapt.

It jumped from two hundred and seventy horsepower to three-seventy between one heartbeat and the next. He could only pray that his rebuild on the small block V8 held.

The Hummer gunned its engine, but Isobel was just plain gone.

By the time the Jeep reached the end of the tunnel, neither vehicle was in sight.

Ricardo's radio squawked as Anton called down from the helo.

"The Hummer went down to the surface streets. Isobel just plain flew out of the end of that tunnel. Damn but that woman can drive."

Devlin looked at the congested highway ahead and figured not only could she really drive—even on a bar bet he wouldn't have tried slaloming through that mess at speed—but she must have nerves of steel.

CHAPTER 15

"*L*ook at this footage!"

Isobel would rather be huddled in the corner of a shower and hiding from the world.

They were back on the houseboat, streaming the three synchronized video feeds of Michelle in the Chevy, Katie in the Jeep, and the helo up above.

The opening sequence and the descent down the hill had come out exceptionally well.

Then the Chevy and Jeep reached the tunnel entrance, and the yellow Hummer showed up like a blot of darkness on the screen. Isobel closed her eyes and it was all she could do to not be sick right on the coffee table.

"He's trained," Hannah remarked softly as the Hummer did its four-wheel drift onto the highway at the beginning of the chase, the last image captured by the helo before all three vehicles disappeared into the tunnel.

Isobel forced herself to look up at the big screen.

"Run it again."

While Ricardo worked the controls, Devlin slid an arm around her shoulders. "You were amazing."

"I was scared shitless," she nodded toward the screen. "Next you're going to tell me how sexy that is."

"The way you drive, oh yeah."

Isobel tried to ignore him, but that arm around her shoulders was all that was keeping the panic-shivers away.

Ricardo hit play and she watched the car handling.

"No," Isobel had them run it a third time despite the churning in her gut. "No. It's none of the Hollywood trainers; the technique isn't one I've seen. I've watched or worked with all the main ones."

They kept watching in silence.

Katie had managed to pan the camera around to capture the Hummer on its first attack on the Jeep.

"Delta?" Ricardo asked.

"SEAL," Hannah corrected him. "See how he handles the moment when I hit the Jeep's brakes? A Delta would have been expecting that move, compensated, and clipped us. They would have had the same training I did."

"What would have happened if he had?" Katie had wrapped a blanket around her shoulders despite the warm evening and Anton practically pulling her into his lap.

Isobel had seen it on a couple of films, but it was Devlin who answered.

"We were going close to eighty at that point. Even with Hannah driving, it wouldn't have been recoverable. A twist and stumble, then a kitty-corner end over end. Even with the roll bars, no survivors."

Hannah looked thoughtful, then nodded at his assessment.

In silence, they watched through the end of Isobel's race out the far end of the tunnel with the nitrous still burning hot in the engine. The helo's camera had followed the racing Chevy, not the Hummer peeling off on the first exit ramp.

"Who the hell was that guy?" Devlin asked in the silence that followed. "And what does he have against actresses?"

Ricardo tapped on the laptop computer. "I took the images Katie captured of him and sent them in. If there's an answer, he'll find it."

"In? To where?"

When no one else responded, Isobel answered him, "To Michael, our commanding officer."

She could see in Devlin's eyes that he was pulling back. Shifting away. And that was far more painful than she'd expected.

"Commanding officer?" He barely whispered it.

"We're independent contractors to a very special team inside the US government."

"You're a military team? What is the actress-thing, just a front? A front for psychics, telepaths, and whatever? Or is that all a lie too?"

His reaction, now that it had kicked in—after they'd become lovers—was the last thing too many, and it tipped her over the edge.

She managed to make it up the stairs and into the bathroom. She managed to lock the door this time, before she simply collapsed onto the tile floor and wept.

~

"You are so not just going to sit there!" Michelle got right up in his face.

"Back off, Red." Devlin didn't know what the hell was going on, but whatever it was sucked.

"You can't just let her walk away like that. You just gutted her."

He'd gutted *her*? He wasn't the one spewing lies here.

"The hell I can't." Even though he suspected she was right

in principle, he didn't need to take on these people's garbage. Some weirdo, psychic, or psychotic filmmakers with delusions of military grandeur. He'd run his life just fine not wallowing in someone else's shit.

Her fist connected with his jaw, hard enough to snap his head aside. He wasn't in the mood to compliment her on her technique. The fact that it appeared to hurt her hand even more than his jaw was a bonus, but not enough.

He put his hand over her face and gave a hard shove.

She flew backward over the coffee table and landed on her back in the middle of the living room. In half a second, she'd scrambled to her feet and crouched ready to charge him.

Anton caught her in mid-leap. Even his six-five and built like a tank was barely sufficient to stop Michelle's rage.

"You may want to be walking your ass out of here right about now, brother. Count-a three I'm gonna unleash her."

"Jesus!" Devlin pushed to his feet and was out the door in two and a half.

A moment later there was a loud smash as something hit the back of the door. Michelle's scream of "Bastard" did not sit well.

Devlin ground to a stop eight steps down the dock. He didn't even make it ten goddamn steps.

He was used to screaming actresses calling him a bastard. They'd crawl into his bed, then expect him to be upset when they walked away. Why the hell should he care? They'd each had their fun. Always seemed to piss them off though.

Except he turned and looked back at the houseboat. Not at the first story, but the second.

Isobel Manella had been more than fun. She'd been incredible. From the moment she'd stepped onto his sailboat, she'd been absolutely fantastic. Temperamental at times, but even then, fantastic.

US military. Why had that thrown him?

It shouldn't have been such a goddamn big surprise. Two ex-Delta Force, who maybe weren't so ex. Two helo pilots with their own personal Black Hawk helicopter. Who had that?

Except Katie was clearly a civilian, just by her going sheet white when he talked about how their Jeep could have flipped. She was in way over her head. And Michelle—he rubbed his sore jaw—for all her fighting spirit, hadn't looked much happier. Paramedic. Not corpsman. Not military medic. Just a standard paramedic.

And Isobel.

Sure she was amazing, but she was still a goddamn civilian.

He thought about his friends from the streets. The Burned Puppies, the Fry Boys, churned out by the US wars in Iraq and Afghanistan. Their brains misfiring so badly they could barely function, never mind hold down a job.

But even the worst of them, suffering from TBI and PTSD so deep they'd never get clear of it in a thousand years, had a code. Part of that code was you don't risk civilians.

And some military commander was sending a woman like Isobel into harm's way? He wanted no part of that fucked-up shit.

But even if he couldn't sense her, he could imagine Isobel's pain.

"Shit!"

He walked back down the dock, jumped up onto the rail, and climbed to the second floor.

CHAPTER 16

The bathroom door handle rattled.

"Go away!" Isobel screamed at it before curling back up on the floor.

There was a click, and Devlin opened it easy as could be.

"You know, these things just have a little pin lock to release them." He shut the door behind him and locked it again.

She kicked at his ankle with her shoe and missed. Instead her shoe flicked off and skittered under the sink.

He slid down to sit with his back at the door.

The ornate tile was cool enough against her butt to send a shiver up her spine. That had to be the cause, because no way was it about him seeing Isobel Manella wrecked there on the floor as if she was a real-life, devastated woman. She never let anyone see her when she was like this, not even Michelle.

"I thought you were gone." Her throat was beyond hoarse. She hadn't wept like that in—since she'd found out Ricardo was going to live after his rescue from torture. But that had been a release. This had been agony.

"Yeah, me too. Guess not."

"Why?" God, she sounded like a frog.

He inspected the ceiling. "Good question. Haven't got a great answer on that one."

"Make something up." After all, that's what men always did.

"Maybe I just want to have sex with you again."

"Fat chance in hell."

He rapped his knuckles on the floor. "Yeah, the tile is kind of hard. Plenty of room in the shower though."

"Dream on."

"Okay. Don't mind if I do," he actually whistled for a moment as if he was doing just that. "You got me in a weird place, Belle."

"Don't call me that."

"Why not?"

"Because I thought it meant something."

This time he hummed a real tune between his teeth.

It took her a moment to recognize the Beatles tune, "Michelle" – *ma belle*. "Two timer."

"Yeah, totally the wrong woman." He rubbed his jaw as if it hurt. "You got me between a rock and a hard place here. I gave up on caring about women long ago, or at least any particular one of you loons. But then I renamed my boat after you and—"

"Ha! I knew that wasn't her name."

"It's painted right across her stern." He must have spotted her total disbelief. "Stayed up all that first night to sand off her old name and paint it new. Even registered the name change."

"You do that for all the women you want to sleep with?"

"Hell no," and he said it so derisively that she actually believed him. "They say it's bad luck to change a boat's name."

"Is it?"

"Jury's still out. I dunno," he shrugged. "It just felt right. I don't have any of your superpowers, but I tend to trust my gut instinct. It just…felt right."

Isobel tried not to be charmed, but wasn't having much luck with it. She forced herself up and leaned her back against the tub.

"You're a real mess, you know that, right?"

She rubbed at her eyes. "I was crying." More like weeping her guts out.

"Shit, Belle. Not talking about that. You could put on a James Cagney mask and you'd still be the most gorgeous person in any room."

"I'm not some lame female who's just going to melt over a compliment."

"You think I don't know that? Not what I was saying anyway. It's just a truth. Just like you being a mess."

Isobel sighed and rested her forehead on her knees. Maybe if she just ignored him, he'd go away.

"You've always been The Strong One since the day you were born, haven't you?"

Against her better judgment, she looked up at him.

Goddamn but the woman had dangerous eyes. So dark and deep a man could get seriously lost in there.

What the hell had he been saying? Something, *anything*, so that he didn't just sweep her into his arms and try to find some way to make it "all better." A ploy that he'd bet would earn him far worse than a sore jaw.

"You've got your six friends pulling at you every which way. The military fuckers breathing down your neck without giving you any of the proper training that you need. Your best friend who wants to treat you like an emotional invalid.

117

Your friend Jennie has thrown your entire career path into question so now you're bankrolling a filmmaking dream you don't even know if you want. Then there's that pain-in-the-ass-sailor temporary-bed-partner who knows he has more issues than Methuselah had kids but never gave a shit about them before. And now some guy with a hard-on to end you permanently. How messed up is that?"

She watched him in silence for a long time.

He could see the thoughts crossing that expressive face. As if he'd just given her a checklist and she was going through them one by one and putting herself back together a little more with each one.

"Name one issue," she finally asked.

"Me?" He waved his hands helplessly in the air. "Just one?"

She waited.

"I dunno. Trust, for one."

"And who was the last person you trusted?"

Sure hadn't been some bimbette actress. He had buddies and pals...but real friends? The kind you could count on like Isobel counted on hers? Not a chance any social worker or any of his foster parents. Some of the guys he used to hang with? No, you didn't trust them, cause when they lost it, they were trained to be lethal.

The last person he'd trusted?

Maybe the first one.

"Belle."

"What?"

He shrugged to indicate that was his answer.

She put her head back down on her knees. "You idiot. Couldn't you pick someone better than that?"

Actually, no, he didn't think he could.

CHAPTER 17

*A*t the soft knock on the bathroom door, Devlin looked up as if he could see who it was through the wood.

"My brother," Isobel offered. Michelle would have just gone for the knob, then tried to kick it in when she discovered the door was locked.

At Isobel's wave, Devlin tripped the lock and shuffled aside far enough for Ricardo to slip in and join them. He simply nodded at Devlin, acknowledgement without surprise. Not much got past him. He silently closed the toilet and sat down. After a glance at her face, he dampened a washcloth in the nearby sink and tossed it to her.

The cool felt good. Like the first hint of relief since she'd felt the man in the Hummer.

"What have you got?"

"Hannah nailed it, ex-SEAL Petty Officer 1st Class Claude Vermette. Disappeared into the SOG for three years. Listed as dead in an explosion that took out everyone and everything at a secret research facility in the Nevada desert a year ago."

"The SOG?"

Ricardo turned to Devlin. "Special Operations Group. The CIA has a division called the Special Activities Division —the SAD. You hear about them heading up the dark missions abroad. The SOG is the SAD's black ops team— sabotage and assassins."

"Our government has assassins?"

Ricardo ignored him and turned back to her. "Rumor is he went SOG, then disappeared even from that."

"Into a research lab," Isobel wanted to hide her face again.

"What kind of lab?" Devlin was leaning forward.

Isobel had to face the one thing she hated most. "He was gifted. It's the only thing that fits. Like he has a psi radar and could feel us. I—" her voice caught in her throat.

Devlin shuffled close enough to take her hand. She found unexpected strength from his grasp.

"I opened up to feel him. You were right, Ricardo. He wasn't angry or afraid. There was no hate. The pieces just don't fit together. Like maybe he was your zealot ready to kill us in pure battle frenzy." She turned to Devlin. "Feelings have colors, sort of. The best way I know how to describe it. You know, black equates with evil, red with anger, and so on. That barely skims the surface, because there's also texture, depth, clarity...but that's the idea."

He nodded for her to continue as if he really was interested and trying to understand. It was killing her that she couldn't see even his base color. Each person had a baseline that remained no matter what emotion lay over it. Michelle wore a burgeoning spring green of kindness that couldn't be denied no matter what chaos her more active emotions were actually in. Ricardo's earth-brown stability was the perfect counterpoint in their relationship, and it was so purely who he was that his emotions rarely varied from that baseline.

"I expected black-evil or red-fury. What I sensed was shining white of such purity and magnitude that I could feel nothing else, not even Michelle in the back seat. As if it was burning hot as a sun compared to normal people. Like one of Ricardo's 'Glory Killers' but with no hatred of the enemy. Of us. I've never sensed true madness before, but maybe that's what it's like."

"Backed up with the skills of a SEAL-trained CIA assassin?" Devlin groaned.

Ricardo sighed and shrugged a yes.

Devlin rocked back, but didn't let go of her hand. "Well, that sounds like a *whole* lot of fun."

Michelle charged into the bathroom, still under full steam.

Devlin had forgotten to relock the door after he'd let Ricardo in.

She spotted him two steps through the door and aimed a hard kick at his face that he barely managed to block. Wouldn't have if she hadn't shed her beloved cowboy boots for bare feet. Instead, he managed to get his forearm up directly in her line of fire.

He didn't hear any toe bones crack, but she yelped hard and collapsed onto the bathroom mat, cradling her toes in both hands. Thank God she was a practical woman who kept her toenails trimmed or he'd be bloody.

A moment later Ricardo said softly, "Because I'm not in the mood."

"In the mood for what?" Devlin asked him.

"My wife just asked why I haven't already killed you."

"Oh. Uh, thanks." Devlin couldn't think of a better response.

Ricardo simply nodded, then laughed softly. "Apparently that makes me a total weenie. My wife's idea of a vile insult."

"Must like me, then. I think she's called me fuckhead, bastard, and a few other expletives in just our short acquaintance."

Ricardo stared at him just long enough to make it clear that the redhead with the fiery temper was his.

Devlin held up his hands palm-out to show that he wanted no part of that.

"Ow-w!" Michelle cradled her toes, then turned her back on him to face Isobel. "I was coming up to tell you that they found the Hummer parked illegally downtown. It was taken out from the dealer for a test drive, using a false ID. The saleswoman was knocked out and tied up in the back of the Hummer. He'd disabled the anti-carjacking tracker."

"There's the proof we needed."

Isobel looked at him in surprise.

"The vets, even the most screwed up ones I've met living on the streets, are still wired up right...on some things. By parking illegally, he made sure that the saleswoman, a civilian, would be found quickly. Bet the windows were even cracked open."

"And that he tried to kill us, also civilians?" Michelle scoffed at him.

"He didn't. That's where the wiring got broken. He has a military code against harming civilians, but also some personal code that invalidates that."

"Hold it!" Michelle looked around the bathroom. "What's his personal code have to do with us?"

"I'm guessing that inside his head you lot—the gifted—don't fall into the civilian category. You're something else in there."

"So what was he doing? Trying to kill us with kindness?"

"Not so much. Though one thing's for certain," Devlin

held Isobel's hand tightly. "He was definitely trying to kill you."

Her hand jerked, then clamped down on his when he didn't release it.

"No," Michelle was shaking her head. "No. That's so wrong. Ricardo, tell him that's wrong."

Ricardo barely hesitated before grimacing.

Devlin hated being right.

CHAPTER 18

Hard bed. Belly full of soup. Another charity mission.

Being dead meant no government draw. More importantly, being dead meant they couldn't find him again.

But he had to find her.

So close.

He'd come so close, but she'd slipped out of his grasp even as he'd closed his fist. Not strong enough. Not fast enough.

His fists clenched until the pain throbbed from them, and still he couldn't be sure it would be enough next time.

He needed more.

His training.

It too had slipped from his grasp. He knew better. Such a simple attack should have worked, but he hadn't been trained to depend on should haves. He'd been trained to deliver results.

"Don't run to your death!" Training had always harped on that. Take the time to plan.

He'd found his target, then acted rashly.

Yes.

But he'd waited long enough.

Now it was time to hunt.
And once he'd found them again, then he could plan.

CHAPTER 19

*I*sobel hadn't felt like sex, but neither had she wanted to sleep alone.

Devlin had made it simple by stating that he wasn't leaving her side. "I'm not as lethal as your brother, but they'll have to go through me to get to you."

He'd sat up against the headboard, fully clothed. He had her Taser resting by his hand, and had showed her the Benchmade knife he carried.

There was little chance that he'd need it, Hannah was sleeping downstairs and her brother out on the deck. Not even Devlin, with an ease that spoke to her of a former life as a night thief, would be able to slip in.

She let herself curl up against him as he gently finger-brushed her hair back from her face, and let herself collapse into sleep.

"What the—" Devlin's flinch brought her wide awake.

A man loomed over the foot of her bed. His shoulders were too broad to be Ricardo's.

Isobel wasn't much given to screaming, but for this man to be here, her brother must be dead.

As she opened her mouth to make her final plea to the gods, the door to the balcony shattered inward.

The man shifted aside into the shadows and Ricardo's attack carried him tumbling onto the bed.

Ricardo instantly rolled back to his feet as Devlin shoved her behind him.

She opened her mind and—

"No! Wait!" Only one person had ever simply been solid-granite gray.

Ricardo and Devlin froze.

The man had somehow crossed the room to the door and flicked on the light switch.

Then he stepped aside half a moment before Hannah shattered Isobel's bedroom door with her shoulder.

Her weapon raised, she scanned the room, aimed at the stranger…then dropped her gun to her side.

"What the fuck!" Devlin was still trying to keep her behind him.

Isobel rested her hand on his shoulder to restrain him, and was impressed that she had that power over him because she could feel his adrenaline pumping.

She knelt on the bedspread, careful of the glass that Ricardo's entry had sprayed into the room.

"Hello, Colonel Gibson."

He nodded his greeting. He wasn't a tall man, the same five-ten as Ricardo. His collar-length brown hair was shot with early gray.

Devlin pushed out of the bed, stepped up to Colonel Gibson, and punched him square in the face.

~

Devlin had him dead to rights. The guy should have dropped like a stone.

Instead, Gibson clamped a hand around Devlin's wrist and stopped his punch cold. If Devlin stuck out so much as a knuckle, he'd honk the guy's nose.

But no cop's cuffs had ever been so firm and secure as the grasp around his wrist. Devlin didn't doubt for a second that if the guy wished, he could simply crush all of Devlin's wrist bones without any visible sign of effort.

"I'm sorry for surprising you. It was necessary to prove that your present security was inadequate."

Devlin looked to see how Ricardo and Hannah took that.

No change in expression. No chagrin. No anger.

It was just a proven fact and he suspected they were both already making new plans.

It was only then that the others stumbled into the room in varying states of undress. The cowboy entered wearing boxers, a Glock 19 handgun, and his hat. Each one spotted Gibson and dropped their defenses immediately.

"Who the hell *are* you?" Devlin still couldn't move his hand.

In answer, the guy handed Devlin Isobel's Taser, which must have been taken from his sleeping hand. "I felt that disarming you was a sensible choice. Your training is different than ours, a true street fighter. It increases your unpredictability—in a useful way." Then he released Devlin's wrist.

"Ours?" Devlin wanted to rub his wrist, but Gibson had cluttered his free hand by returning the weapon precisely when he had. Besides, there was no need. He'd been stopped with no pain inflicted, simply as immobilized as if Devlin's fist had been cast in concrete.

Gibson nodded toward Hannah and Ricardo. "Two of my very finest soldiers."

And that, finally, earned him a reaction from the two ex-Deltas. Surprise?

Gibson held out his hand. "I'm the former commander of Delta Force, Mr. Devlin Jones. I'm pleased that Isobel's heart has found such a staunch champion. Her instincts are as exceptional as ever."

This time it was Isobel who reacted with surprise.

Ricardo just smiled, "Pretty obvious, sister."

"But I— We— All we did was go sailing."

Gibson's nod toward the rumpled sheets had the urge to punch this guy return tenfold.

"As I said. A champion," Gibson stared straight at him. "A pleasant surprise considering your history. Well done." He scanned the two shattered doors. "Shall we retire downstairs and discuss next steps?"

"Shall we back up a second and talk about you being an asshole?"

"Do you think I don't protect my team?"

"Yes, that's precisely what I think, you arrogant prick. And three of them are civilians, not a 'team.' Still like to fix your goddamn face for putting them at risk."

Gibson studied him and Devlin refused to look aside. But neither did he speak.

The former commander of Delta Force. And his statement that Ricardo and Hannah had been two of his very best. The very best of the most elite fighting force the world had ever seen.

Maybe he didn't take his duties so lightly. Plus he was here.

No, he wasn't just here. He'd walked by two of his "best" and disarmed Devlin in his sleep. Devlin was *not* a deep sleeper—a habit of self-preservation from his time in the Children's Home Society orphanage, two very rough foster homes out of the five he'd been in, and a couple spins through juvie that had been bad enough to finally scare him straight.

Yet none of that had stopped this Gibson. He must have been a field man before he was a paper pusher. If they made a field guy into the commander, that probably meant he was *the* very best.

Then Devlin felt a chill up his spine.

"This guy? You?" If a man of this caliber was here, then what did he know about the man who'd attacked them? A matchup between a crazy CIA assassin and an aging Delta Force commander?

And Gibson's face darkened. "His skills are exceptional. And based on where he was incarcerated..." his uncertain shrug did more to prove his worth to Devlin than any tricky ninja shit. He wasn't just blowing smoke because it would be easy and more comfortable to hear.

Gibson must know that this guy was seriously bad news, which was precisely why he *had* come to Seattle despite Ricardo's and Hannah's presence. Okay, maybe not a total asshole.

"Oh, here." Gibson handed Devlin his Benchmade knife before turning for the door.

Devlin had to slap his back pocket to make sure it was his.

How the hell had he done that?

CHAPTER 20

"*You're crazy!*"

Colonel Gibson merely smiled. "That's been posited by many people before you."

Isobel could feel the control slipping through her fingers. For a year she'd managed to assemble and run this team.

She also knew that it was Gibson who had found Jesse and Hannah for them.

But then he'd placed himself in charge of the team's missions without so much as a by-your-leave to her. Of course, that's when she'd found out he'd been running them from behind the scenes all along anyway.

Devlin's words still rankled as well—the truth of them.

Jennie, with the best of intentions, *had* thrown Isobel's professional life into complete turmoil. As the actress, she knew who she was, what her purpose was. To take the script that a writer had created, and become a vehicle to embody the director's vision of those words.

Now, as co-director and producer, she couldn't immerse herself in the role as she so typically enjoyed doing. She was known for keeping in character for the entire duration of the film—which had caused difficulties on some of the darker films she'd done early in her career. Thankfully, her rising star gave her the power to turn down those roles now.

This film was turning her into a complete scatterbrain. As an actress, all she'd had to field were scripts, auditions, and calls for her to be a line model for some product she'd never used so she wouldn't endorse.

Suddenly she had distributors bidding on the project, advertising campaigns to plan, and—because she'd chosen to run it lean—an entire film crew to wrangle without five layers of managers and unit directors to fend them off.

Somewhere in there Devlin hung out, clear enough in her peripheral vision, and far too clear when she turned the lens directly upon him.

Her personal life might have been depressingly bland, but that had also made it easily manageable. Even the paparazzi had become bored with her—mostly. They certainly hadn't bothered to find her in Seattle yet.

Gibson's assessment was easy to ignore. But for her eminently practical brother to agree, to sanction Devlin as a good match for her was...

"You're all crazy!"

"It's the only scenario that makes sense," Gibson insisted. "You have to keep making this film."

"You want to use Isobel as bait?" Her champion still hadn't backed down and she wanted to kiss him for it.

Gibson rubbed his forehead for a moment. "Perhaps we should try this. You are a practical man, Mr. Jones, with an interesting variety of skills, from camera work to peacemaker. Yes, I had someone interview some of the vets still living near your former haunts."

Isobel was shocked at the risk she'd taken stepping onto this stranger's sailboat. In taking him to her bed. She knew nothing about him.

"Now," Gibson was still focused on Devlin. "Battlefield tactics. How do you protect a VIP target?"

"You get them the hell out of there."

Gibson nodded. "But that won't prevent the adversary locating that target at a later time. Not when the VIP is as prominent as Ms. Manella and the aggressor as skilled as Mr. Vermette. So what do you do then?"

"I sure as hell don't use her as bait."

Gibson sighed, but Isobel was starting to see the pattern so she spoke up.

"Bait is when someone is out there on their own, appearing helpless. If I'd been alone in that car, he'd probably have gotten me. But I wasn't. The helo told us he was military. Hannah's presence distracted him, and her driving skills bought me enough time to get clear. The more I surround myself with the trappings of a movie, the more protected I become. On a normal film, there are layers of security to make sure that the public can't get to me. They even prevent distractions from other film crew members. We just have to wrap me in enough protection that he can't get to me. A film naturally puts me at the center of that protection."

"No!" But she could see Devlin thinking. His eyes flicked around the room quickly before refocusing on her. "Jesus, Isobel. The risk…"

She brushed a hand over his cheek. Maybe Gibson and Ricardo were right. She might not know much about Devlin Jones, but maybe, just maybe it would be worth taking the time to find out more.

There was no question in her mind that he was seeing her, Isobel Manella. Not any of her roles, not even the playful lover enjoying herself during their first nights together. He genuinely feared for her.

Devlin had signed up to be a local tour guide for site selection, and a general handyman for the shoot. For the first time, he was thrust into the middle of the maelstrom that was a film.

They gave him the title of Production Manager, which meant that somehow it was now his problem to make the whole thing happen.

And because they weren't willing to risk any civilians outside the Shadow Force team, other than himself, the real film crew was put on hold "pending script changes."

To replace the personnel, this Colonel Gibson had called in some favors.

By the next morning, a pair of military war dogs were on site with their handlers: a big bruiser of a guy with one real arm and one artificial, and a lovely brunette who was just as serious as he was and wielded just as big a dog.

They arrived in a small helo flown by a lovely blonde whose greeting proved that someone had found a heart inside Colonel Michael Gibson. Devlin's personal jury was still out on that being possible.

Another ex-Delta couple, who apparently owned a major vineyard just a few hours south in Portland, Oregon, showed up next.

A sniper from the national Hostage Rescue Team named Kee arrived on "vacation time."

Assorted others filtered in.

Many waved greetings, traded heartily thumping embraces, and showed off photos of kids and dogs.

Over the next twenty-four hours, Devlin was kept too busy to do much thinking. Instead, he taught each new arrival their various roles on a film to go with their security responsibilities. His history of filling in where needed on prior films was suddenly very handy. He assigned people to whatever seemed a decent fit: props, logistics, equipment rental from the local theater supply outfit, a striking blonde named Emily took over the catering. Oddly, she received more respect than anyone else there. Neither Jesse nor Anton could even speak in her presence, which Devlin rather enjoyed watching.

He couldn't keep all of them straight. So, he taught them what he could and told them to come find him if anything went sideways.

He expected catastrophe.

Instead, they blended in as if they really were a trained film crew. The questions that did reach him were intelligent, and typically more about verifying an answer they'd already come up with than needing one. It was hard to remember that these were highly trained military elite, deeply skilled at blending in and adapting quickly. More than that, these were the people who owed Colonel Gibson a favor and answered his call. That meant the bar was set up at some serious level of competence.

No one was told about Shadow Force: Psi's capabilities; Gibson kept that to the inner circle, though it was pretty clear that the blonde cook knew as well. As far as everyone else was concerned, there was a rogue SOG assassin after one of Colonel Gibson's friends. Apparently that was enough for them to drop their lives on no notice and filter into Seattle from around the nation.

Frankly, it was a damned impressive demonstration of Gibson's concern and power.

It was also a little terrifying that he felt it was needed.

Devlin himself and Shadow Force: Psi became Isobel's buffer from all the mayhem.

The only place that was completely sacrosanct was the houseboat. No one knew its whereabouts except Gibson.

Before departure or return, Anton and Katie would take ten minutes to "check things out."

As far as he could tell, they just sat there holding hands.

"What are they doing?" He'd whispered the question to Michelle.

"Being freaks like the rest of us."

"Jesus, Red, get the goddamn stick out of your butt. I'm just as worried as you are."

She'd actually rested a hand on his arm in apology: her biggest concession since he'd tried to walk away from Isobel and only made it eight steps down the dock.

"Just forget it." But when he went to leave, she held onto his arm. So he waited her out.

She cleared her throat a couple times before starting, as if nervous to be talking about any of their skills. Hard to blame her with some crazy CIA guy hunting them.

"Anton may be a kickass helo pilot, but he can also send his vision lookabout. He is sitting there," she nodded toward the couch, "but his vision is walking all of the streets around the area."

"The chance of him seeing this guy… Hell, we don't even have recent photos of him. Just that one image Katie caught on film."

She shook his arm as if telling him to shut up. "That's what Katie is doing. She can't feel emotions like Isobel. But she *can* feel when someone has been somewhere. Ricardo said she's one of the best trackers he's ever met even without her gift. With it, once she's felt someone, like she did with this jerk when he almost crashed into her, she can tell Anton if he crosses their track again. He and Katie have to be in contact for it to work, but if Anton does cross the guy's path, she can tell him how to follow it."

"Slick. So, Claude Vermette can't get near the place without us knowing."

"We don't think so. Anton and Katie tried following you and it worked, despite the weird block you have against Isobel."

Devlin felt an itch between his shoulder blades.

Michelle laughed at him. It wasn't a kind laugh. "Not enjoying your time with the freaks?"

"You know, if you keep calling yourselves that long enough, you're gonna start believing it. It's not how I see you, so you should stop seeing yourselves that way."

"Bull pucky, Devlin. I saw you flinch because they followed you, asshole."

He turned to face Michelle. "You're not Isobel."

"Duh!"

"What I mean is…" Devlin scrubbed at his face, trying to straighten out his own thoughts. "Don't think that *you* know what the hell I'm feeling."

"It was on your face, jerk." Her nails might be short, but that didn't stop them from digging into his arm.

"On my face—" Christ but he didn't want this memory back but he couldn't think how else to explain it. "You ever been hungry, Red?"

"Before every meal."

"No, I mean bone hungry. So deep that the pain in your gut makes you cry no matter what you tell yourself?"

The answer to that was clear.

"In between times the system snatched me up, I knew that hunger. I'd beg, borrow, steal, fence. Didn't matter."

Michelle's wide eyes said he'd just walked way outside her experience.

"My reaction, my flinch, was for the fear I felt when I *knew* that the cops had eyes on my sorry ass. Back when no amount of hiding, or even just turning around and seeing no one there, could convince that poor, starving kid he was in the clear."

He slowly peeled her fingers off his arm and hissed as the blood flow restarted.

"I hope to God you never feel that. I damn well hope I never do again either. So, don't think that you know what I'm thinking. Even if I wasn't somehow blocked from her, you're not Isobel. You can't read shit about me."

Devlin wasn't ready for what he saw in her eyes. It wasn't disgust or distrust. It was compassion and pity so deep that he couldn't stand to look at it.

Instead, he turned to watch Anton and Katie watching somewhere else.

Michelle patted his arm a couple times where she'd clawed him. Then she leaned her forehead against the side of his shoulder. He wasn't ready for the hot moisture of tears filtering through his t-shirt.

Damn Isobel for being right. He patted Michelle's hand now resting lightly on his forearm because he didn't know what else to do. As prickly and temperamental a bitch as she could be, at her core Michelle was a total sweetheart.

CHAPTER 21

or three days, as the layers of shielding built up around her, nothing happened.

Because she didn't know what else to do, Isobel leaned into the film as a safe haven and complete distraction. She buried herself in the work.

The film was set to take place in a single day in her character's life—one that would change her forever.

They'd gotten a lot of usable footage for the final car chase. Acquiring the yellow Hummer had guaranteed they'd have the vehicle if they needed it. But she'd made it clear that she wasn't going to drive it.

The dealer had offered it at a bargain as Claude Vermette had dinged it up too much for it to be sold as new. Then Devlin, being smart, had offered them a screen credit and they'd given it to the film for free. If it survived, they wanted to have it back to resell "as seen in the latest Isobel Manella film." Fine with her, as long as she didn't have to touch it. She could almost feel Vermette's psychic madness lingering in its chassis.

She'd also refused to drive the reshoot of the passage

through the downtown tunnel. Instead, Devlin had done the drive wearing a wig and slouching lower in the seat to Isobel's height.

All that morning, she'd huddled in the houseboat with her protective ring around her.

No one had bothered him and she felt foolish for her refusal, no matter how much Devlin insisted otherwise.

Gibson hadn't been so very wrong about him being her champion. He was fearless of anyone. He plagued Ricardo with what-if questions until she thought her brother would go mad. Then Devlin would ask something Ricardo hadn't thought of, and in moments Hannah and Gibson would be called in for a change in some tactic in the security perimeter she couldn't stand to think about. Never in her entire career had she been so cut off from the world around her.

Devlin had also proved his bravery when he faced Michelle down about being too overprotective. And he was always willing to listen to Jennie with the patience that she sometimes so required.

So, she took her cue from that, and let him handle all of the headaches.

Because the film was to occur over a single day, and they were shooting in order, the shooting schedule progressed a little later each day.

And by the third day, they'd settled into a routine.

The main floor of the houseboat had become command central. Extra workstations had been set up and one television screen was now four that could be fed separately or as one monstrous image.

Lunches were soon crowded into the kitchen or out on the back deck as the dining table now belonged to the camera and sound gear.

Once clear of the dawn sequences, they started their

mornings with final shot planning and logistics. Then there was the day's shoot sequence.

Back at the houseboat, they reviewed that day's film.

She and Jennie would spend hours making notes on the useable sequences and a rough edit of how it all fit together. A Delta operator named Richie became her remote editor. At the end of each day, she'd send off the pan, zoom, and splicing instructions of what shot to use from each camera. Each morning, they could watch the rough cut on the footage.

Actually not so rough. She'd been hoping for a viewable rough cut because video editing and cleanup was an incredibly technical process. But by the third day, he was returning near usable film. There was no planned CGI, and she'd wanted a gritty reality so his finished product was very close. It was definitely something she could send to a finish editor as a master template.

When she'd let him know that he was that close, he'd re-rolled all the way through the first couple days' work bringing everything up to his new standard. Along with the note, "My wife, The Cat, has a really good eye. Two actually. Isn't she awesome?"

They both were...and she hoped to meet them someday, but they were outside the protective bubble that Gibson had built around her.

Once the daily edit sheet was shipped to Richie, she and Jennie would plunge into polishing up the next day's master storyboard. Gibson's team would use those to plan and implement tomorrow's setups. Even at her level, it wasn't very often she could step on a set and perform, but they were so efficient that there were minimal delays.

The only relief was when she plunged into bed. Sometimes Devlin was still out working with the teams. Other times, he was already passed out facedown. But they always woke curled up together, which was a pleasant surprise every single time.

"When are we going sailing again, Devlin?" she whispered one morning as they lay curled up and watched the dawn light catch first on Queen Anne Hill's trio of radio towers across the lake.

"Once you're safe, Belle. Then I'll take you anywhere. We can take her up to the San Juan Islands north of here. Better yet, I'll borrow a friend's cruiser so that we can sleep aboard. A fifty-foot sloop with blood-red sails, you'll love it. We'll head up the Inside Passage past the Canadian Gulf Islands. There are quiet inlets where you can swim and no one would know you're there."

"You trying to get me naked, Beast?"

"I can take care of that right now, Belle," and he tugged on the hem of her nightshirt, but she stopped him when she heard Ricardo and Michelle up and chatting in the next bedroom. Quiet nighttime talk or lovemaking didn't pass through the walls. But once daytime routines were going, there was very little privacy in the packed houseboat.

Devlin placed his face between her breasts and groaned in frustration.

As she dug her fingers through his unruly hair, she had a thought.

Frankly, they'd expected an attack almost immediately, yet there hadn't been one.

She didn't want to stop the filming, but today, even shooting out of order wouldn't get them around the one problem she hadn't dealt with.

Unless...

Devlin was going to hate it, and she couldn't wait to tell him!

$\sim$

Devlin decided that soul-deep exhaustion wasn't such a bad thing when you got to bury your face between breasts as incredible as Isobel Manella's. The thin nightshirt hid nothing and added that little tease of something to peel off the woman…soon. It was one he'd bought for her that said, *Life is just a series of obstacles that keep you from sailing.*

There was a brief silence.

Maybe Michelle and Ricardo were done. Then he heard a dresser drawer slam next door. Michelle's unsubtle signal for them to get moving. "Next time, Belle, we get a houseboat to ourselves. Deal?"

"Deal." She fooled with his hair a bit more. "I have this great idea."

"If it isn't telling everyone else to go to hell and letting me just keep you in my arms the rest of the day, I don't want to hear it." He was getting damned sick of life's little obstacles to their sex life.

He felt her happy sigh. "Please keep thinking that way."

"I guarantee it." Because her words meant that thinking about it was all he was going to get to do.

She wrapped her arms around his neck and a leg over his hip, pulling him tight against her, which either made it worse…or better…or both.

He held her just as tightly while the damn woman purred. He hadn't known that women could purr, but Isobel could. A low soft thrum deep in her chest, making that perfect cross between utter contentment and raw sexuality.

"You know today's shooting sequence."

He knew it. Or he had in his role as Production Manager. He couldn't seem to bring it to mind with the pleasant distraction of their current positions.

"The rest of the cast and crew isn't actually due for two more weeks."

Civilians had to be kept safe. He gritted his teeth, *some* civilians did.

"And you know that put my on-screen partner into a schedule conflict."

He nodded and enjoyed the sensation of doing so while being enveloped in Isobel.

"That means..." And she trailed off.

That meant that today's shooting schedule, where her character Rosamaria was actually interviewed and hired at a small private investigator firm in Pioneer Square, couldn't be shot. That interview was the pivotal moment that would launch her from out-of-work job applicant into fighting side-by-side with her new boss for their very lives. There was no more film—except during brief moments in the action sequences and when the hero was brutally injured near the climax so that Isobel could face off the killer alone— when the two of them were apart.

Still Isobel didn't say a thing. Just her gentle fingers fooling around in his hair making his hormones try to transcend mere bodily residence.

Almost as if she was enticing him to—

"Hold it."

She giggled. Ms. Sophisticated Always-perfectly-controlled-under-any-circumstances Isobel Manella had just giggled at him.

He pushed away enough from pure heaven to open his eyes and inspect her face.

"If ever there was an evil smile—"

It just grew bigger. She was clearly delighted with some joke.

And he suddenly knew to the pit of his gut that's exactly what it wasn't.

He reburied his face against her chest and groaned.

CHAPTER 22

"I didn't sign up for this," Devlin protested as Isobel did his makeup in the bathroom. He needed very little to accent those features for the camera. It was hard for Isobel not to trace them with her fingers as she did the work.

"As one of the leads, you'll get paid handsomely," she reminded him.

"I don't want your money," he grumbled as Michelle tried to help him out of his normal clothes. "Back off, Red."

"Spoilsport," Michelle shot Isobel a wink she couldn't help returning.

With his t-shirt already peeled off, a half-dressed and very frustrated Devlin Jones was indeed a very pretty sight.

"Holy crumbs!" Michelle had circled around behind him, and was now staring at Devlin's grand, multi-colored dragon tattoo. She poked it, almost as if testing to see if it was alive.

He turned far enough to swat Michelle's hand aside.

"Plus a percentage of the profits," Isobel reminded him.

"Not gonna be any of those with me on the screen." He looked terribly uncomfortable in the button-down shirt.

"Don't you ever wear a decent shirt?" Michelle tried to restraighten the collar he'd mussed in under thirty seconds.

He looked down at it. "Never. T-shirts in the summer and turtlenecks in the winter. That's it."

Isobel rested a palm on his bare chest to calm him down. She needed him to do this. Though it was hard to ignore the temptation to shoo Michelle out of the bathroom and take Devlin up on that shared shower idea. Imagining him in a form-fitting turtleneck as black as his hair was a very attractive idea. Still being together for the change of seasons? That she was less sure about.

"Maybe his dragon would be comfortable in a decent shirt. Can't we cast it instead of this useless louse?" Michelle just couldn't leave it alone.

"Red!" Devlin growled out.

"There!" Isobel knew it when she saw it. "That's the baseline for your character. Not just your normal salty self, but think of having to deal with Michelle instead of me."

"Nightmare," he grunted out, but grinned at Michelle.

"Utter and total," Michelle agreed with a matching smile. "Okay. What if... Wait a sec." And she rushed into the bedroom. She came back with an armful of the clothes that Devlin had brought over from his place to save time.

"No...No...No..." She began tossing bits and pieces of his clothing aside onto the floor.

Devlin just sighed in exasperation.

She held up one to his chest, looked at his face, then tossed it aside as well. She held up another and let out a lascivious wolf whistle. "Put this on."

Isobel looked and decided that, as ever, Michelle knew her clothes.

Devlin pulled on an ocean-blue t-shirt that made his blue eyes shine. Across the front was a pictogram of the evolution of man: chimp, ape, early man with a sharpened stone, upright man with a spear…and a sailboat.

"Sexy, competent, gives the character some depth, especially if we never mention the sailing in the script. And he's stopped squirming like a three-year-old in a suit."

"Go to hell, Red."

"You'd look damn good in a suit, jerk. Nothing too modern, probably a Brooks Brothers. In gray I think. Or a—"

"No chance."

Isobel slid up to him and rested a palm on his chest. It was all too easy to picture him in a suit. Leave his hair long, and definitely keep that couple-day beard that made him look rugged even as it accented his features.

"This is a good look on you, Devlin. And you're comfortable in it, so we'll go with that. Though go with the slim leg black jeans that Michelle picked out."

~

Sucker!

It was all Devlin could think as he sat waiting at the same Merchants Cafe table where he'd had lunch with Isobel before all of this got so real.

Michelle and Katie were tucked back in the shadows with their cameras.

But the Isobel who strode in wasn't the lovely actress in the sundress. Her hair was wet and bedraggled as if she hadn't bothered to do a thing with it after a shower. She wore battered jeans, faded white in places, and a loose camo jacket that revealed her form under a tight, plain-white tank top in bare glimpses. Battered Army boots completed the image.

Rosamarie Cruz dropped into the seat across from him before speaking.

"You Roscoe?" Her voice said she cared about as much as shit on her shoe if he was or wasn't.

"You gotta be kidding me. You're Cruz?" He didn't need to feign his surprise. It was almost impossible to recognize Isobel, though she wasn't hidden from view.

Her shrug of "Whatever." She *was* that disillusioned, out-of-work ex-soldier.

And his head was in the script. He knew the damn thing cold. All of the setups and planning sessions, frame-by-frame storyboard reviews with Gibson's people, holding Jennie's hand when she needed it—they'd all burned the thing into his brain.

"Beer?" It was just eight a.m. script time.

Again that shrug. How could she express so much emotion with so simple a movement?

He signaled Tammy at the bar with two fingers.

The two of them studied each other in silence while they waited and the cameras waited with them.

Devlin had to remind himself that this wasn't some military burnout. This was a woman putting herself in harm's way to find someone who wanted her dead. She had a core of strength that both showed—yet didn't in the character before him.

Sure, Rosamarie Cruz had the experience, but she didn't have the confidence to go with it. Like Isobel in some ways. He wasn't sure he'd ever met a woman more skilled in more ways. She'd had to be. Actress, team leader, dealing with her friends' and her own gifts, and a society that would freak if they knew about them. Yet she was totally convinced that she was screwing up on every front.

Tammy thunked the beers down on the table, no coasters though they were on her tray.

"My tab," he grunted at her.

Tammy just rapped her knuckles on the table and waited.

"Shit!" He dug out his wallet and handed her a twenty.

"That covers the interest, you still owe me for the beers. This ain't your office, Roscoe." She stuffed the bill into the back pocket of her tight jeans and strode back off screen. Yeah, easy bet he wouldn't be getting that double sawbuck back, ever.

"Big spender," Rosamarie grunted out, then slugged back half the beer with the ease of a drunk. It was easy to forget this sloppy woman was Isobel.

He drank enough of his own beer to match her. At least Tammy had given them a good draft, a Freemont Golden Pilsner.

Rosamarie jammed her hands back in her jacket pockets and slouched.

"You got any skills?"

She pulled a fist out of her jacket. He heard a sharp metallic snap as she flicked her wrist. Faster than he could blink, she had done the necessary release-flip-twist-and grab to unfold a Bali-Song butterfly knife. She held it for half a second directly in their shared line of sight—long enough for him to recognize the Benchmade 85 Billet Ti. Six hundred and fifty dollars of knife. To any aficionados, it would make a statement on screen that the character carried that class of a weapon.

And it made a hell of a statement about Isobel. First, that she'd practiced its tricky handling enough to make it look natural. Second, that he was lucky to have survived walking into her bedroom uninvited.

Then, with an effortless flick, she sent it whistling past his ear to thwap into a wooden post close behind him.

He turned and inspected its perfectly perpendicular placement before pulling it free and flipping it closed once more, without nicking himself. He still had the moves—a street thug never forgets. Then he tossed it back to her. She caught it midair and it disappeared back into her pocket.

Her smug smile at surprising him, with the knife and the skill to use it, fit both Isobel and Rosamarie.

Remembering his role, he lifted his beer and finished it. Then he shoved to his feet. There were a couple more lines, but he realized they didn't need them.

"Interview's over."

Isobel/Rosamarie didn't move. He liked the surprise and confusion on her face.

"You coming?" Devlin/Roscoe called as he headed out of the bar.

The pause, then fast scrape of her chair on the old wood floor was all the answer he needed. When he heard the sound of a quickly emptied beer glass being slammed back down on the table, he decided maybe he was in love.

Not really, but that tiny detail of not wasting half a beer was such a perfect touch of finesse for a down-on-her-luck character.

Once out of sight of the cameras and around the corner to the stairs, he turned to wait for Isobel's reaction to his attempts at the role.

She hustled out of the bar, and when she saw him standing and waiting, she walked straight into his arms.

"Little early in the script for Roscoe and Rosamarie to get it on," he managed. "Was that okay?"

"This," she squeezed her arms around him, pressing their bodies tightly together, "is all about Isobel and Devlin. Roscoe was perfect, by the way!"

"You'll need to reshoot all of this, you know? When you get a real actor."

"Not a chance!" She dragged him down and kissed him hard.

Maybe this movie gig wasn't so bad.

CHAPTER 23

The tension kept climbing with each day and Isobel didn't know how much more she could take. Today had been their longest day yet. As the movie's "time of day" had shifted later, the shooting times had moved with it so that the light would be right. But everything around it hadn't shifted.

The morning reviews of finished film and preparations for the day's shooting were getting more complex as the movie was becoming more complex. Despite returning later and later from each day's shoots, there were still the dailies to review, the editing plan to make, and storyboards to update for the next day.

The shoot was going better than she could ever have imagined. When they botched a single take, they just kept filming as they reset and continued. The flow was close enough to seamless. She'd planned a twenty-day shoot across the city and by today, Day Eight, they were well ahead of schedule. The final sequence at the Opera House had been scheduled for four days, but it might well take only one or two at the rate they were moving.

Of course, filming more scenes faster than planned only added to all of the schedule pressures. More film meant longer review-and-edit sessions, more storyboards had to be checked for the next day, and all the rest of it.

That was aside from the acting.

Devlin was a natural for this role, he *was* Roscoe in so many ways. Gruff, untrusting, far too used to being on his own. His growing dependence on Rosamarie's highly trained awareness was as unrealized as his own growing attachment to her.

There was no longer any way to tell what was real between them and what was their characters. The line between their real lives and their roles blurred more and more.

Rosamarie needed Roscoe to pull her back from the cliff edge of despair. And both Rosamarie and Isobel needed Devlin like she'd never needed a man before in her life.

Did he need her? Or was he just doing the film and being her White Knight before he drifted off to his boat and cars to wait for whatever came next?

And on top of all that, they were making absolutely no progress on finding Vermette.

Twice she'd caught "whiffs" of him. Both times she'd been in the car between the filming location and the houseboat—thankfully nearer the former than the latter. If she lost the sanctuary of the houseboat, she just might pull the plug on everything and run.

But as soon as the feeling of the hard-burning whiteness was in range, it had been gone again. Just passing by at a distance.

And Isobel couldn't stay open all of the time. She'd go crazy trying to scan and feel all of the thousands of Seattleites around her.

She also wouldn't be able to act her way out of a B movie with such distractions inside her head.

They'd filmed following a lead down into the Seattle Underground.

A meetup on a cross-Sound ferry, except it was a "corpse" not an "informant" who had awaited them.

They'd followed clues and done the race through the steam tunnels. They'd found the dead—carefully bloodied warriors from Gibson's people—but never quite catching up with the unseen assailant.

This afternoon they'd finished with shooting in Seattle's Old Town. Tomorrow would be the car chase back up the northbound tunnel as Rosamarie was slowly forced to return toward her point of origin that very morning at the apartment atop Queen Anne. She had to arrive there a changed woman.

What was surprising was that Isobel could feel herself changing.

Jennie's original script hadn't contemplated any relationship forming between Roscoe and Rosamarie, especially not in a single day. But they were two wounded souls: him trusting no one, and her convinced that she needed no one because she could never find anyone to trust. And the synergy between them hummed on the dailies every time they reviewed them.

But how much of that synergy was Roscoe and Rosamarie and how much was Devlin and Isobel, she could no longer tell.

"I've got something," Devlin slid an arm around her waist. "Are you up to keep going?"

She leaned into his embrace for a long moment and just closed her eyes and let herself feel.

Isobel still couldn't feel him.

But she could feel herself.

Could feel the whirlwind of conflicting emotions that had been churning inside her all day were suddenly quiet. Could feel that it was Devlin's influence.

Could feel the question inside herself that she'd felt Hannah, Michelle, and Katie each in turn ask themselves.

Could she love this man?

"You ready?" Devlin asked softly.

"Yes." And she felt no surprise at her answer.

She turned enough in his arms to kiss him. *Very ready.*

Devlin led Isobel and the others to where he'd heard some of his old friends had moved, up underneath the I-5 overpass along 6th Avenue.

"I used to hang with these guys," he kept Isobel close by his side. "At least some of them. Soldiers who fought for their country but can't seem to do more than survive on the streets." He could see that other homeless lived there, but they avoided the loose enclave of the vets.

"So much pain!" Isobel had jolted against him. The impact of their emotions so strong he was almost afraid she'd scream. That wouldn't go well at all here.

But she wrestled down the urge. By the easing of her breathing, he knew she'd shut off that inner sense again.

It took a bit of jogging some memories, but Devlin was soon welcomed back into their circle, as much as an outsider ever could be. He even managed to get their permission to film them.

Michelle and Katie did a great job of blending in with their cameras.

He couldn't see the circle of protection that he hoped Gibson had pulled around them. But he could see the vets tense up, then relax. Like recognizing like perhaps. It told him that the security perimeter was in place.

It took only the slightest suggestion to Isobel for her to stay in her Rosamarie role.

She didn't turn on the charm, which would have shut them down. Instead she was just a slightly earthier version of herself. It was more to her credit than his own that they relaxed into telling their tales. Some were chilling, some were just retelling of times gone by.

But Isobel had taught him enough to be able to sift through the dialog and see the scene.

Roscoe and Rosamarie squatting in the darkness, lit by distant streetlights and the background flash of headlights on the massive concrete columns around them.

Bit and pieces, tales and hints, perhaps cut together as a chaotic montage. He fed them a few lines, so that their tales became a hotbed of clues about the man Roscoe and Rosamarie were tracking across Seattle.

But as he listened, he realized that he was getting more than he'd asked for.

There actually was a shadow moving through Seattle that the vets weren't willing to talk about directly. Claude Vermette had left an impression behind him that was uncomfortable to even the toughest warriors.

This was film he'd have to study very carefully.

Afterward, Isobel had tried to pay them with no success. It was her only mistake in the whole evening. They'd brushed aside the offer. Rosamarie had been accepted into their circle and you didn't take money from a sister or brother inside that circle.

But the caterer had known what to do.

While they'd been having their talk, Emily had set up her food truck and cooked a meal for them. Bowls of pasta with mushroom-pepper sauce, burgers of top sirloin, and a big spread of homemade apple and berry pies. It was some of the best food Devlin had ever eaten on a shoot, squatting under the roaring concrete overpass.

The guys had been more respectful of Emily than even the best mission volunteers.

It was only as she was packing up and he was thanking her that he saw her trying to rub the red out of her eyes.

"Are you okay?"

The lovely blonde had shaken her head no. "Two of them used to be in my command. Not my flight crew, but good people. It breaks my heart." She climbed into the catering truck and was gone before he could think what to say.

"In her command?" Devlin whispered to Isobel close beside him.

She nodded and looked infinitely sad. "How do we really thank them?"

Devlin smiled at that. "That one's easy." He called out, asking who ran the best soup kitchen around.

Typical homeless, they couldn't just say. It was part of how they passed the time. It was also an important question to them, where was the best place for a free meal. Even though the answer was clear from the beginning, it took a pleasant half-hour's debate before they settled on their answer.

Rosamarie had simply nodded.

Even though it was now nearly midnight after an exhausting day that had started at dawn, Isobel had insisted they go past the place.

She gave them a check for fifty thousand dollars and her card. "If you ever can't feed everyone who comes here, you call me."

Now it was Devlin's turn to try to rub the red out of his eyes.

CHAPTER 24

*H*iding.
  So hard.

It hurt to hide inside. But it had worked.

"No gain without pain," his commander had always said. "Get comfortable being uncomfortable."

He'd squelched himself, though it was near agony.

Don't think. Don't feel. Close down so that nothing remained except the searing pain where they'd ripped him away from himself.

It was worth it.

It had worked and he'd found them.

Found her.

Eaten their food.

Heard their plans for tomorrow.

"No plan survives first contact with the enemy."

She wasn't the enemy, but she was definitely the target.

He'd be ready.

He'd save her from that hellhole in the Nevada desert.

Because even death was better than going back.

CHAPTER 25

*T*he day was off to a strangely slow start.

Isobel was downstairs and halfway through breakfast before she missed Devlin.

"He's off with Colonel Gibson," Michelle set a bowl of fruit and yogurt before her, then came back with two mugs of coffee. "Apparently they were up half the night sifting through last night's film and wanted to go check something."

"Did he say what he found?"

Michelle just shook her head. "What did *you* find?"

Isobel considered. "Humility? Maybe?"

"Huh?"

"We, Shadow Force: Psi, we've danced in and out of a dozen different assignments, little the worse for wear. Sometimes better," she smiled at Katie as she sat down across from them with her own bowl. They'd found her by accident during a mission.

Hannah came into the house. She looked like she'd just run a fast 10K. She poured herself a massive glass of OJ, drank half of it back, refilled it and then sat beside Katie.

"We're learning humility this morning," Michelle told the others.

"About time," Hannah grunted out.

"What do you mean?"

Hannah toyed with her glass, staring down into it as she twisted it back and forth on the tabletop.

"Those soldiers last night, they gave too much, didn't they?" Isobel prompted her when she didn't speak.

Hannah shrugged. "They gave what they gave. I've never met a soldier, not even glory-hound whack-jobs, who thought there was anything good about war. At least not after the first real battle. But if they'd given any less than they did…" Again that shrug, but she didn't look up. "Would they be dead? Or their team? Or some civilian they were protecting? They gave what they gave."

"What about us?" Michelle's voice sounded small as she rested her palm on her belly. "Are we supposed to give more? How can I if I'm a mother? I can't do that, can I? You can't ask me to do that."

Hannah shook her head. "I'm not. No one is. But we have special skills. When they can be applied to advantage, we'll use them. There are problems out there that we can solve like no others, or I wouldn't be here. Humility is knowing there are problems out there that we *can't* solve, no matter how much we'd wish to."

Now she looked up for the first time and studied each of them in turn.

"You three are civilians. I had five years of training *before* Delta would even test me. We do what we can safely do. Safely. Every Delta soldier has the choice to abort the mission if we deem it too dangerous. We're trained a lot in how to make that judgment."

"What about Isobel? How does she judge?"

Isobel had known Hannah for a year and only now felt as if she was getting to know her.

Hannah turned from Michelle and faced her. Her green eyes looked sad.

"Sometimes," her voice was so soft that Isobel had to lean in to hear her. "You run out of choices."

~

"Squat."

Gibson nodded his agreement.

"Bupkis. Diddly. Nada."

Gibson narrowed his eyes at him and Devlin shut up.

The threads had all been there, it had just taken him most of the night to weave them together.

By the time he and Gibson had reached the vets' camp, most of the guys had already dispersed for the day. They'd be off begging, hanging out at the library, or just squatting somewhere else for a while. The few they were able to corral were, by definition, not the most together ones—or they'd have gotten out and about.

One guy thought he might have recognized Claude Vermette from last night's chow line, but that was the best they had.

"If he was here, why didn't he try to attack?"

Gibson chewed on that one for a while before answering.

"If it was because he saw the scale of protection we had here, that would be the good scenario."

"How big a scale was it?"

"We had the full team. You weren't trained to see it, but they were here. I'd theorized that he might have had contact with the local vets. I should have left a man here, but I didn't."

"Why didn't Isobel sense him?" Then Devlin remembered. "Never mind. She said there was too much pain here and must have switched it off. So you think we might have scared him off?"

"Why do you say that?"

"You said that if he left her alone, it was because of your protection detail. That's a good thing, right?"

Gibson shook his head. "The bad scenario is that Claude Vermette was listening and planning. His failure to act earlier, or last night, would be typical if he was observing and studying his target prior to acting."

Devlin felt far colder than was justified by the foggy morning.

"And I suspect that he doesn't want to simply shoot her. That some part of him must need to do it personally, perhaps to be sure it is done. Just as he destroyed the facility where he was incarcerated."

And that was another worry. "If they had *him*, might they send out a team to capture Shadow Force to study? We can't take on the whole CIA. Do they know that if they're ever caught, none of them would ever see the light of day again?"

"I have tried to mitigate that risk as much as possible. There are backup plans to protect or recover them if I should ever fail, but that's all they are—plans. However, I have been looking into current risk and there is hope. I have reason to believe that Mr. Vermette destroyed that facility as it was being visited by the project directors as well as all the scientists. They were set to demonstrate something, or had a breakthrough. Claude appears to have awaited his moment, survived somehow, and managed to kill them all at once. I have some associates at the NSA. While they all agree that it was a CIA black site, they assure me that no one knows what that project was, not CIA, FBI, DIA, or any of the others."

"So Claude is free and safe, but doesn't know it."

"And probably would never believe it either. He also believes that Isobel is either a threat or…"

"Or what?"

Gibson didn't speak again, even after they were back in their car and headed once more for the houseboat.

"Out with it, you've got something stuck in your craw," Devlin pushed at his silence.

"I fear..."

The fact that the former commander of Delta Force used that word definitely gave him the creeps.

"...what if Mr. Vermette's madness isn't to kill Isobel? Or not exactly? What if his goal is to *save* her?"

CHAPTER 26

"We ready?"

"Every day is a new day." Isobel did her best to smile. Devlin and Gibson had both been very quiet upon their return. When asked if they'd found anything, Devlin had shaken his head no, then shrugged as if it was a "maybe" that he wasn't comfortable with.

"Too bad it's nighttime," Devlin was sitting in the passenger seat of "Rosamarie's" '57 Chevy.

Eleven p.m. on a Tuesday night.

They'd worked through the day. Prepared both of yesterday's sessions for Richie. Tonight's storyboard should be simple. They were just doing the car chase from Pioneer Square, up onto the ramps, through the tunnel, and finishing at the Seattle Opera. Tomorrow they'd start the final scenes inside the Opera House.

"Aw shit!" Devlin's curse was emphatic enough to make her jump and look around frantically.

"What?"

"It's Tuesday. For the second time in two weeks, I missed the Duck Dodge. They're going to think I died."

"You go to every one?" Isobel tried to remember how to breathe. She really didn't want to drive the tunnel again, even if it was in the other direction. They simply didn't have enough footage of the Hummer and had to rerun the scene. And the footage they had of her only showed the one passenger in the car. The script required two as she was now teamed up with Roscoe.

"First two races I've missed in three years."

Isobel tried to imagine what that was like. To be somewhere that she could do that. She rarely knew where she'd be month-to-month. She'd given up the house in San Antonio and bought a condo to store her stuff. But films were shot on location or in massive studios like Pinewood or Baja or Mammoth. In its entire history, San Antonio had about three dozen films that included scenes there. Seattle boasted well over two hundred and Vancouver, Canada, just a few hours north, had shot almost six hundred.

Neither one was Hollywood, but neither were they San Antonio.

Maybe it was because it was the city she'd been raised in, but San Antonio didn't hold much attraction for her. Seattle had the movie scene, an incredibly active theater scene (she hadn't done a stage play since Texas A&M), restaurants, sailing, Devlin…

No! It was just because they were shooting this crazy, dangerous movie together. That's all it was.

She'd fallen for a costar once. It had blown up first in the media, then in real life. An ugly mess that had led each of them to turning down roles—good roles—if the other was in the movie.

There was no reason to believe there would be any relationship once the movie was a wrap. In fact, there was every reason to believe there wouldn't be. He'd made that clear so often she almost believed him.

Almost.

Which was a world apart from thinking there *might* be a future with him?

She wasn't even sure what the question was anymore.

Isobel almost yelped with relief when Jennie had Ricardo announce that they were finally ready.

~

Devlin's palms itched to be at the wheel but, for the film, it wasn't his car.

He watched the leads roll out.

The city had come up with a variation to his rolling roadblock model, but they still had to keep it tight.

Flashing road signs had been posted announcing: "Possible Delays—up to 10 minutes."

First the cop cars who'd be making sure the tunnel was clear. After that came the general traffic. Which couldn't be civilian traffic, of course. But he'd contacted the local stunt driver school and they'd agreed to make it the graduation exercise for their latest master class.

Once they were well dispersed through the tunnel, and instructed to hold their lane and relative position precisely so that Isobel and the Hummer could weave through them at speed, it was their turn.

"Do it up, Isobel."

"That's Rosamarie to you, boss."

Once again, Michelle was slouched in the back seat with a camera. This time Ricardo was driving the film Jeep and Hannah was at the very rear, driving the Hummer. She had on a dark wig and they'd raised the seat enough that she'd look like Claude Vermette in a high-speed night shot.

Jen signaled them off the mark.

Isobel gunned the engine and popped first gear hard enough to smoke the tires.

She didn't ease up the entire way up the curved on-ramp.

"Jesus," Devlin hung onto the door's armrest. "This is a top-heavy tank, not a Lotus. Don't roll it."

In answer, Isobel popped the next gear and kept up the pressure.

He was leaning as far as he dared into the curve when she hit the end of the ramp and jumped between the first cars. To make the motions look real, they hadn't slowed down the "traffic," instead running it at fifty through the tunnel. She was into third gear and doing eighty by the time she had to volley between lanes to clear the first group of vehicles.

He caught a glimpse of the bright orange Jeep in the passenger's side mirror—the addition had been one of his few concessions to modern safety. That and shoulder belts. The nitrous system was an exact copy of a 1958 mod kit he'd found, so he didn't count that.

Then he spotted the Hummer.

On the next lane change, he saw the Hummer coming hard. Harder than it was scripted to.

"Hannah's on a tear, Rosamarie. Keep your pretty ass moving."

Isobel drove like she was riding the tail of a twister, clearing one car after another by inches.

The three key vehicles were supposed to come together in a choreographed gap so that the Hummer could swing around the Jeep and the camera could then follow it into the next set of cars, chasing their Chevy.

Instead, the Hummer cornered the Jeep behind a Toyota pickup, and blew past on its right side.

"Shit, what is Hannah doing?"

"Talk to me," Isobel called out. "I can't take the time to look behind me."

"It isn't Hannah," Michelle called out. "Ricardo, in the Jeep, said that it wasn't Hannah. It's *him.*"

CHAPTER 27

*I*sobel opened herself up for just a split second.

It was a near fatal mistake.

The blazing white of the Glory Killer was so much brighter than the first time that she was momentarily blinded.

She cut it off just as Devlin grabbed the wheel and jerked it sideways so that they could career between a Jetta and a Camry.

Isobel took the wheel back. "It's definitely him," she managed to gasp out.

"You guys really need a telekinetic to unplug that guy."

"The best we've got is for Hannah to throw a sonic boom, but she needs Jesse for that and... Oh God, if he's there, where's Hannah?" Isobel took her foot off the gas to go for the brake.

Devlin stomped down on top of her foot hard enough to hurt, pinning both her foot and the gas pedal to the floor.

They blew through the gap where the passing was supposed to happen at over a hundred miles an hour. He yanked out the Overdrive that would ease the engine back from redline at such speeds. A 1957 third gear simply wasn't all that deep.

She plunged into the second phalanx of traffic.

Deep in the tunnel, no police were going to serendipitously appear on the scene. The front sweep team would have cleared the tunnel by now, and the follow-on team was ordered to stay well behind so that they weren't captured on camera.

They were passing through the low point, two hundred feet underground and a hundred below sea level. No convenient helicopter was going to save them.

"Are there any big trucks ahead?"

Devlin had taken his foot off hers, but didn't answer. Which was the answer. She'd have seen them in the queue.

"Did you recharge the nitrous bottle?"

"No. How long did you run it the first time?"

"I wasn't exactly counting seconds; I was more running for my life." A memory that Isobel had hoped to never, ever, under any circumstances repeat.

"I doubt if you could have run more than twenty seconds or you'd have launched into orbit. You should have maybe a minute more, five or six ten-seconds thrusts, still in the bottle."

Isobel looked at the massive grill of the Hummer that was fast filling up her rearview.

"It's set to trigger whenever I put my foot to the floor?"

"Exactly." Devlin leaned down to crank open the valve on the nitrous bottle on the floor under her seat. "Once we hit that arming switch, a wide-open throttle will fire it." When he was done, he kissed her on the thigh.

She really hoped this wasn't goodbye.

Again she delayed the Hummer's attack by dodging around a couple of the slower moving cars.

"He seems to have decided that hitting anyone else will delay him too much."

"Good thing for our helpers. Bad for us."

She found a bit of straightaway and shouted out. "Hit it, Devlin!"

~

Devlin barely remembered the next few minutes. It was all chopped into snapshots.

An opening, Isobel hammering the throttle, and the old Chevy leaping through the gap. There were no straightaways, they'd intentionally mixed up the traffic.

After one or two seconds of jarring acceleration, she backed off the throttle and the transmission whined, but it held.

From the backseat, Michelle was calling out the approaches of the Hummer. In watching behind, she swung the camera around for a whole series of trailing shots.

The Production Manager part of Devlin's brain fully approved. His desire to live through this decided he was nuts for caring at all.

"Transition lights!" The overhead tunnel lights ahead were dimmer indicating the end of the tunnel just as they ran out of traffic to dodge behind.

The Hummer closed the gap fast.

The police had parked across the highway lanes just past the exit to guide them onto the turn for the Opera House.

"No way through." In a car as old as his Chevy, there simply wasn't the safety equipment to survive crashing through the blockade.

Isobel punched down on the gas. With a roar, the nitrous oxide dumped power into the engine and the Chevy leapt again. He wondered how much more the engine could take.

"It's not going to be enough room to do this," Isobel shouted out.

"To do what?"

"I'm sorry, Devlin."

For killing him? Yeah, he was sorry too.

Isobel stood on the brakes.

The Hummer plowed into the rear of his car, crumpling the tailfins and trunk. It also knocked them partly sideways.

Then Isobel dropped down a gear and punched the accelerator again.

With a nitrous driven roar, she shot sideways into the L-sharp turn of the exit. It was a perfectly executed move.

The Hummer overshot and plowed into one of the cop cars.

Just as Isobel took the next of the three right turns to head them to the Opera House, the Hummer slammed into reverse, then raced after them—but it was now a block behind.

"Shit, woman, you *can* drive."

"The police are just standing staring at the wreckage," Michelle called out. "Don't know whether to poop in their pants or the hats."

Sparks began glancing off the Hummer's hood and windshield.

Gunfire.

Devlin finally heard the roar of the big Black Hawk over the roar of the Chevy's V8.

That sniper, Kee, was up with Anton and Jesse.

But the Hummer wasn't slowing down. Even the civilian versions were tough.

Another turn and they were on Mercer Street, the city street headed straight to the Opera House.

Isobel tromped the throttle one last time.

Thankfully, the street was mostly empty at ten at night.

"Where do we go?"

Devlin had been thinking about that. Running hadn't worked all that well.

"What if we stopped running?"

Isobel glanced at him, then offered him a tight smile. "Worth a try."

"Take your next left. Then a hard right at the end of the road through a chicken wire gate onto the Opera's loading dock."

He reached out to pat his poor car's dashboard and hoped to God this worked.

CHAPTER 28

*I*sobel took the sharp left just before the Opera House, then raced down the back alley with Vermette's Hummer close on her tail.

She did her best to remember how far it was to the gate because she couldn't afford to slow down. With a sharp twist of the wheel and a brief yank on the emergency brake, she got fully sideways in a four-wheel drift. She dumped the brake and gunned it again.

The Chevy smashed through the gate and raced up the loading dock ramp. Three of the four big loading doors were blocked with delivery trucks, but the fourth was open and she gunned ahead. Hitting it at over sixty.

The door blew inward as they were slammed painfully against the seatbelts. Blown off its tracks, the door flapped up and they drove beneath it, through the Stage Left area, and plowed onto the set at the tail end of four long skid marks.

Silence. Except for the hollow creaking as the broken trunk lid continued to rock up and down.

She was suddenly in a massive forest of towering fifty-foot trees rising out of the rocky ground.

A dragon with a head bigger than her car was glaring at them through the windshield.

"Okay, that's different." Michelle must still be alive.

"What the hell?" Devlin was staring up as well.

Isobel had looked forward to seeing this production. "Wagner's Ring Cycle. That's Fafner. He builds castles for gods and guards magic gold."

"Uh, hi. Don't mind us," Devlin waved at him. Then he turned to Isobel, "I prefer *my* dragon, personally."

"Me, too."

A loud crash sounded off to the right and the trees shivered and swayed. The Hummer must have hit the back.

They dove out of the car and circled around Fafner.

"Shouldn't we be running the other way?" Michelle asked softly.

"He might still have Hannah in there from when he snatched the Hummer," Devlin led the way. He'd even freed a crowbar from his poor wreck of a car. No matter how disaffected he claimed to be, his loyalty and concern for others just shone out of him. He wanted to know what was sexy? It wasn't sailing a boat or driving a car. It was that he was willing to stalk a trained killer to help one of her friends.

The Hummer was lodged into the back of the set's towering latticework of aluminum frames that supported the massive fake trees.

Numerous holes had been punched through the Hummer's hood, roof, and windshield, but the door was open and the driver was gone—except for a trail of bloodstains.

"Check the back," Devlin ordered as he scanned the area.

Isobel began to panic when there was no one in the back seat.

Inside the back hatch, Hannah lay on the floor. Duct tape over her mouth and bound with rope both hand and foot. But she was wide awake and looking absolutely furious.

Isobel flicked out Rosamarie's Bali-Song blade and cut her bonds.

The first words she croaked out were, "Where is that bastard?"

~

Devlin kept circling, but couldn't spot the blood trail anywhere. Then he looked up from the floor and there it was on the framework, just at eye level.

He followed it upward. More blood.

Vermette had climbed the latticework of the set to the very top of the artificial forest. From there, large chains led farther up to a fly loft another five stories higher than the forest set piece.

At the top of the trees, there was a human shape lost in the shadows.

Vermette hadn't been able to climb the chains. Too exhausted? Too injured?

The four of them gathered at the base and looked up at him.

"Come down, Claude. We can help you," Isobel called aloft.

"He's set on killing you, you know?" Devlin felt that really needed to be kept in mind.

"It doesn't matter. If we can help him, we sho—"

"They're coming for you!" Claude shouted down.

"Who?"

"Them! They'll come and scrape the life and soul out of you!"

"No, Claude," Devlin remembered what Colonel Gibson

had said about the lab. "You got them all. When you destroyed the Nevada lab, you got them all."

"Someone knows!" His voice rose to a howl.

"No. We checked. Everyone who knows was there that day. You got them all. You completed your mission."

There was a long silence from above.

Isobel slipped her hand into his and held on.

"No!" The shout was sudden and abrupt. "They'll find you! They'll hurt you in ways you never can understand. The pain lives. The only safety is in death."

Then Devlin saw Claude stand high atop those artificial trees—and leap!

Yanking on their clasped hands, Devlin jerked Isobel aside.

Claude landed facedown and didn't move again.

A knife was still clenched in his fist, its point driven deep into the stage floor mere inches from Isobel's feet.

CHAPTER 29

*E*veryone agreed with Devlin's suggestion that they could use all the film of the chase and the crash on the Opera House stage, but nothing of Claude himself.

Once the police were gone and the rest of the team had assembled on the opera stage, they re-staged a different final scene.

Devlin called in the opera's technical crew, but he knew that once they removed the vehicles and started repairs, the rest of the footage would become unusable. The final scene needed to be shot amid the wreckage.

With the opera crew's help, they planned a final chase within the Opera House and filmed it straight through the night.

Anton, with his massive six-foot-five football player frame filled in for the mad killer. His final death wasn't from a fall—which had been the original plan as well as Claude's demise—but rather from the crew teaching Rosamarie how to make the dragon spit twenty-foot propane-driven flames.

The last five days of shooting had become one.

Now, there was only one more scene to film.

He found Isobel on her knees scrubbing at Claude's bloodstain. Actually, scrubbing at where it had been, because she'd long since cleaned it up.

Devlin pulled her away, leading her by both her hands.

"It's almost dawn, Isobel," he wiped away her silent tears. "I think we need to be done with this film. Want to go for a drive?"

He led her out to the loading dock as the opera crew began fixing their damaged set. The shot-up Hummer was gone. A couple of the crew had battered his car back into drivable shape—kind of. The Jeep was parked safely to the side. The sky was just turning the softest pink.

She nodded a little robotically.

He waved a hand at Michelle and Katie, who shouldered their cameras and began filming.

"You ready to go home, Rosamarie?"

At her nod, he tucked her into the passenger seat and started the Chevy. The body metal rattled and banged as he drove, but the car still ran.

∼

"Hey, Rosamarie?"

Isobel turned to look down at Roscoe from halfway up the apartment steps at the top of Queen Anne Hill where she'd started the filming less than two weeks earlier.

Downtown Seattle was a sun-washed backdrop behind him. Below lay Lake Union. A few sailboats were out on the quiet blue waters. God but Devlin made a picture leaning against the hood of his battered old Chevy with his arms crossed over his chest and that brilliant dragon's wing just showing on his biceps.

She'd always have to remember him like this. The man,

the lake, and his beloved boat. It was a memory she'd cherish wherever the future led her.

"You make sure you fix my car up good or I'll come after you." She stopped halfway up the steps, angled to the camera so that the dawn light just caught her hair.

"Ever been sailing?"

"Rosamarie" could only shake her head. That wasn't the next line. Roscoe was supposed to make the question just as casual but ask, "See you tomorrow?"

She was supposed to think about it, then say, "We'll see." before walking into the apartment building that had opened the movie.

Maybe end the film on her walking away. Maybe on his knowing smile, trusting that she'd be back. She and Jennie had both liked the power of the slightly enigmatic ending.

Instead he'd asked...

There, between those crossed arms, he still wore that bloody and tattered t-shirt. The evolution of man from chimp to sailboat. And it still fit him like he was a work of art.

Despite his mirrored shades and her inability to read his emotions, she could read his smile.

He might be asking "Rosamarie" one question, but he was asking Isobel Manella an entirely different one.

Devlin Jones. A future with Devlin Jones? Somehow in the last ten days she'd gotten to where she couldn't imagine one without him.

"Sailing?" He repeated the question, then tipped his head as if calling her back to the car.

She hated the endings of movies. Not the story, but being the actress in the last shot. Then it was over. The excitement, the people, the challenge would be done and gone, and she'd feel adrift.

Maybe there was a chance to finally continue the story past the last clapper.

Isobel cocked a hip as Rosamarie thought about it, but she didn't think too long. Together, she and Rosamarie strolled back down the steps.

She stopped a toe's breadth from Roscoe/Devlin.

Too damn self assured, he was just waiting for the ending kiss.

Instead she held out a hand, palm up.

He looked down at it, then smiled a question.

"Keys. I'm driving."

He dug them out and dropped them into her palm. "Just try not to ding it up any worse."

She scoffed at him.

Then, together, they climbed into the twisted and mangled car, and both cameras followed them as they headed down the hill to go sailing.

EPILOGUE

*D*evlin had thought it was corny, but coming out of the premier at Seattle's Cinerama theater, he knew that Michelle had been right.

"You're a crazy romantic, aren't you, Red?"

Her cowboy boot clipped his ankle, but not too hard. Probably because her baby bump was six months out and it threw her a little off balance. Hannah was just starting to show. Devlin imagined himself with a baby of Isobel's riding on his shoulders and couldn't wait.

He grabbed Michelle and gave her a kiss on her temple. "That ending was great. The *Belle* just sailing away across the water with the two of us on board. Then the pull back and up with the helo. Real sweet, sister-in-law."

"Eww! So not!" She shoved him away and wiped at her arms as if trying to dust off his cooties. "I'm not related to you until tomorrow's wedding. I still get another twenty-seven hours of freedom."

"You're a *hell* of a maid of honor, Red." Twenty-seven hours to heaven.

"The threat still stands, sailboy. You hurt her and I'll—"
She squawked in surprise as Ricardo swept her aside.

They'd be flying out in the morning to the Montana
ranch where Gibson lived. Isobel had shot a film there and
swore by it. They'd invited Gibson's impromptu film crew,
and no one else. The Oregon vineyard was providing the
wine, the ranch was catering, and Kee-the-sniper's teenage
daughter had cooked them up a "so retro but whatever"
soundtrack for dancing that was just perfect.

There was a big round of applause as Isobel and Jennie
came out of the theater arm-in-arm. Co-directors and co-
writers, he wanted it to be about them rather than the "Big
Screen Couple" that the rags were already chattering on
about.

But once they'd done their photos and bows, Isobel had
beckoned him over for a threesome photo. He'd caved on the
gray suit. But not the shirt.

Just as he stepped in between them to slip his hands
around both of their waists, he unbuttoned his jacket and
brushed it open to expose it for the cameras.

What had looked like a printed tie with the jacket closed
was revealed to be the top of a sailboat's sail. The revealed
words made a simple declaration.

Yes, we have a plan. Sailing.

The laughter rolled through the crowd.

After Jennie drifted away, already deep in writing their
next film, Isobel placed a palm directly over the photo of the
Belle at the center of the shirt before leaning in to kiss him.

The press went wild, but with the beating of Devlin's
heart against her palm, Isobel didn't care.

She'd spent a whole career being careful about who she
was seen with and doing what. Kissing Devlin Jones after the
premier of her first movie as producer was too perfect to

pass up. Even if the wedding wouldn't be announced until it was over and done.

Granted the audience had been heavily Seattle-based, but they'd given the film hoots and cheers, so she had hopes that it would play well.

Now there was only one place she wanted to be.

On *their* houseboat.

She'd purchased the big one, which had a big enough slip alongside it for the *Belle.* Isobel had also bought three other houseboats along nearby docks so that her team of friends would always be close.

"But not too close," as Devlin often said.

The downstairs of their houseboat was perfect for parties and to use as the primary meeting room for *B&B Films.* Someday their children would play together there. The upstairs was all hers and Devlin's.

People could ask all they wanted, but she and Devlin hadn't explained the meaning of the new company's name to anyone.

Everyone, even Michelle, incorrectly assumed that at least part of the name was for *Belle* the boat.

"Take me home, Beast." Isobel clasped Devlin's hand in both of hers and slipped the golden duck First Place sticker from their first race together into his palm.

He stared at it in their cupped palms for a long moment, then closed his grip over it so that they were both holding it.

"Can't wait, Belle."

$\sim$

Be sure to keep reading to see an excerpt from the exciting White House Protection Force series.

IF YOU ENJOYED THAT,

YOU'LL LOVE THE WHITE HOUSE PROTECTION FORCE SERIES!

OFF THE LEASH (EXCERPT)

"*Y*ou're joking."

"Nope. That's his name. And he's yours now."

Sergeant Linda Hamlin wondered quite what it would take to wipe that smile off Lieutenant Jurgen's face. A 120mm round from an M1A1 Abrams Main Battle Tank came to mind.

The kennel master of the US Secret Service's Canine Team was clearly a misogynistic jerk from the top of his polished head to the bottoms of his equally polished boots. She wondered if the shoelaces were polished as well.

Then she looked over at the poor dog sitting hopefully on the concrete kennel floor. His stall had a dog bed three times his size and a water bowl deep enough for him to bathe in. No toys, because toys always came from the handler as a reward. He offered her a sad sigh and a liquid doggy gaze. The kennel even smelled wrong, more of sanitizer than dog. The walls seemed to echo with each bark down the long line of kennels housing the candidate hopefuls for the next addition to the Secret Service's team.

Thor—really?—was a brindle-colored mutt, part who-knew and part no-one-cared. He looked like a cross between an oversized, long-haired schnauzer and a dust mop that someone had spilled dark gray paint on. After mixing in streaks of tawny brown, they'd left one white paw just to make him all the more laughable.

And of course Lieutenant Jerk Jurgen would assign Thor to the first woman on the USSS K-9 team.

Unable to resist, she leaned over far enough to scruff the dog's ears. He was the physical opposite of the sleek and powerful Malinois MWDs—military war dogs—that she'd been handling for the 75th Rangers for the last five years. They twitched with eagerness and nerves. A good MWD was seventy pounds of pure drive—every damn second of the day. If the mild-mannered Thor weighed thirty pounds, she'd be surprised. And he looked like a little girl's best friend who should have a pink bow on his collar.

Jurgen was clearly ex-Marine and would have no respect for the Army. Of course, having been in the Army's Special Operations Forces, she knew better than to respect a Marine.

"We won't let any old swabbie bother us, will we?"

Jurgen snarled—definitely Marine Corps. Swabbie was slang for a Navy sailor and a Marine always took offense at being lumped in with them no matter how much they belonged. Of course the swabbies took offense at having the Marines lumped with *them*. Too bad there weren't any Navy around so that she could get two for the price of one. Jurgen wouldn't be her boss, so appeasing him wasn't high on her to-do list.

At least she wouldn't need any of the protective bite gear working with Thor. With his stature, he was an explosives detection dog without also being an attack one.

"Where was he trained?" She stood back up to face the beast.

"Private outfit in Montana—some place called

Henderson's Ranch. Didn't make their MWD program," his scoff said exactly what he thought the likelihood of any dog outfit in Montana being worthwhile. "They wanted us to try the little runt out."

She'd never heard of a training program in Montana. MWDs all came out of Lackland Air Force Base training. The Secret Service mostly trained their own and they all came from Vohne Liche Kennels in Indiana. Unless... Special Operations Forces dogs were trained by private contractors. She'd worked beside a Delta Force dog for a single month—he'd been incredible.

"Is he trained in English or German?" Most American MWDs were trained in German so that there was no confusion in case a command word happened to be part of a spoken sentence. It also made it harder for any random person on the battlefield to shout something that would confuse the dog.

"German according to his paperwork, but he won't listen to me much in either language."

Might as well give the diminutive Thor a few basic tests. A snap of her fingers and a slap on her thigh had the dog dropping into a smart "heel" position. No need to call out *Fuss—by my foot.*

"*Pass auf!*" *Guard!* She made a pistol with her thumb and forefinger and aimed it at Jurgen as she grabbed her forearm with her other hand—the military hand sign for enemy.

The little dog snarled at Jurgen sharply enough to have him backing out of the kennel. "Goddamn it!"

"*Ruhig.*" *Quiet.* Thor maintained his fierce posture but dropped the snarl.

"*Gute Hund.*" *Good dog,* Linda countered the command.

Thor looked up at her and wagged his tail happily. She tossed him a doggie treat, which he caught midair and crunched happily.

She didn't bother looking up at Jurgen as she knelt once more to check over the little dog. His scruffy fur was so soft that it tickled. Good strength in the jaw, enough to show he'd had bite training despite his size—perfect if she ever needed to take down a three-foot-tall terrorist. Legs said he was a jumper.

"Take your time, Hamlin. I've got nothing else to do with the rest of my goddamn day except babysit you and this mutt."

"Is the course set?"

"Sure. Take him out," Jurgen's snarl sounded almost as nasty as Thor's before he stalked off.

She stood and slapped a hand on her opposite shoulder.

Thor sprang aloft as if he was attached to springs and she caught him easily. He'd cleared well over double his own height. Definitely trained...and far easier to catch than seventy pounds of hyperactive Malinois.

She plopped him back down on the ground. On lead or off? She'd give him the benefit of the doubt and try off first to see what happened.

Linda zipped up her brand-new USSS jacket against the cold and led the way out of the kennel into the hard sunlight of the January morning. Snow had brushed the higher hills around the USSS James J. Rowley Training Center—which this close to Washington, DC, wasn't saying much—but was melting quickly. Scents wouldn't carry as well on the cool air, making it more of a challenge for Thor to locate the explosives. She didn't know where they were either. The course was a test for handler as well as dog.

Jurgen would be up in the observer turret looking for any excuse to mark down his newest team. Perhaps teasing him about being just a Marine hadn't been her best tactical choice. She sighed. At least she was consistent—she'd always been good at finding ways to piss people off before she could stop herself and consider the wisdom of doing so.

This test was the culmination of a crazy three months, so she'd forgive herself this time—something she also wasn't very good at.

In October she'd been out of the Army and unsure what to do next. Tucked in the packet with her DD 214 honorable discharge form had been a flyer on career opportunities with the US Secret Service dog team: *Be all your dog can be!* No one else being released from Fort Benning that day had received any kind of a job flyer at all that she'd seen, so she kept quiet about it.

She had to pass through DC on her way back to Vermont —her parent's place. Burlington would work for, honestly, not very long at all, but she lacked anywhere else to go after a decade of service. So, she'd stopped off in DC to see what was up with that job flyer. Five interviews and three months to complete a standard six-month training course later— which was mostly a cakewalk after fighting with the US Rangers—she was on-board and this chill January day was her first chance with a dog. First chance to prove that she still had it. First chance to prove that she hadn't made a mistake in deciding that she'd seen enough bloodshed and war zones for one lifetime and leaving the Army.

The Start Here sign made it obvious where to begin, but she didn't dare hesitate to take in her surroundings past a quick glimpse. Jurgen's score would count a great deal toward where she and Thor were assigned in the future. Mostly likely on some field prep team, clearing the way for presidential visits.

As usual, hindsight informed her that harassing the lieutenant hadn't been an optimal strategy. A hindsight that had served her equally poorly with regular Army

commanders before she'd finally hooked up with the Rangers
—kowtowing to officers had never been one of her strengths.

Thankfully, the Special Operations Forces hadn't given a
damn about anything except performance and *that* she could
always deliver, since the day she'd been named the team
captain for both soccer and volleyball. She was never
popular, but both teams had made all-state her last two years
in school.

The canine training course at James J. Rowley was a two-
acre lot. A hard-packed path of tramped-down dirt led
through the brown grass. It followed a predictable pattern
from the gate to a junker car, over to tool shed, then a truck,
and so on into a compressed version of an intersection in a
small town. Beyond it ran an urban street of gray clapboard
two- and three-story buildings and an eight-story office
tower, all without windows. Clearly a playground for Secret
Service training teams.

Her target was the town, so she blocked the city street out
of her mind. Focus on the problem: two roads, twenty
storefronts, six houses, vehicles, pedestrians.

It might look normal...normalish with its missing
windows and no movement. It would be anything but.
Stocked with fake IEDs, a bombmaker's stash, suicide cars,
weapons caches, and dozens of other traps, all waiting for
her and Thor to find. He had to be sensitive to hundreds of
scents and it was her job to guide him so that he didn't miss
the opportunity to find and evaluate each one.

There would be easy scents, from fertilizer and diesel fuel
used so destructively in the 1995 Oklahoma City bombing,
to almost as obvious TNT to the very difficult to detect C-4
plastic explosive.

Mannequins on the street carried grocery bags and
briefcases. Some held fresh meat, a powerful smell
demanding any dog's attention, but would count as a false

lead if they went for it. On the job, an explosives detection dog wasn't supposed to care about anything except explosives. Other mannequins were wrapped in suicide vests loaded with Semtex or wearing knapsacks filled with package bombs made from Russian PVV-5A.

She spotted Jurgen stepping into a glassed-in observer turret atop the corner drugstore. Someone else was already there and watching.

She looked down once more at the ridiculous little dog and could only hope for the best.

"Thor?"

He looked up at her.

She pointed to the left, away from the beaten path.

"Such!" Find.

Thor sniffed left, then right. Then he headed forward quickly in the direction she pointed.

Clive Andrews sat in the second-story window at the corner of Main and First, the only two streets in town. Downstairs was a drugstore all rigged to explode, except there were no triggers and there was barely enough explosive to blow up a candy box.

Not that he'd know, but that's what Lieutenant Jurgen had promised him.

It didn't really matter if it was rigged to blow for real, because when Miss Watson—never Ms. or Mrs.—asked for a "favor," you did it. At least he did. Actually, he had yet to meet anyone else who knew her. Not that he'd asked around. She wasn't the sort of person one talked about with strangers, or even close friends. He'd bet even if they did, it would be in whispers. That's just what she was like.

So he'd traveled across town from the White House and

into Maryland on a cold winter's morning, barely past a sunrise that did nothing to warm the day. Now he sat in an unheated glass icebox and watched a new officer run a test course he didn't begin to understand. Lieutenant Jurgen settled in beside him at a console with feeds from a dozen cameras and banks of switches.

While waiting, Clive had been fooling around with a sketch on a small pad of paper. The next State Dinner was in seven days. President Zachary Taylor had invited the leaders of Vietnam, Japan, and the Philippines to the White House for discussions about some Chinese islands. Or something like that, Clive hadn't really been paying attention to the details past the attendee list.

Instead, he was contemplating the dessert for such a dinner that would surprise, perhaps delight, as well as being an icebreaker for future discussions. Being the chocolatier for the White House was the most exciting job he'd ever had.

~

Keep reading at fine retailers everywhere:
Off the Leash

ABOUT THE AUTHOR

USA Today and Amazon #1 Bestseller M. L. "Matt" Buchman started writing on a flight south from Japan to ride his bicycle across the Australian Outback. Just part of a solo around-the-world trip that ultimately launched his writing career.

From the very beginning, his powerful female heroines insisted on putting character first, *then* a great adventure. He's since written over 60 action-adventure thrillers and military romantic suspense novels. And just for the fun of it: 100 short stories, and a fast-growing pile of read-by-author audiobooks.

Booklist says: "3X Top 10 of the Year." PW says: "Tom Clancy fans open to a strong female lead will clamor for more." His fans say: "I want more now...of everything." That his characters are even more insistent than his fans is a hoot.

As a 30-year project manager with a geophysics degree who has designed and built houses, flown and jumped out of planes, and solo-sailed a 50' ketch, he is awed by what is possible. More at: www.mlbuchman.com.

Other works by M. L. Buchman: *(* - also in audio)*

Thrillers

Dead Chef
One Chef!
Two Chef!

Miranda Chase
Drone*
Thunderbolt*
Condor*
Ghostrider*

Romantic Suspense

Delta Force
Target Engaged*
Heart Strike*
Wild Justice*
Midnight Trust*

Firehawks
MAIN FLIGHT
Pure Heat
Full Blaze
Hot Point*
Flash of Fire*
Wild Fire
SMOKEJUMPERS
Wildfire at Dawn*
Wildfire at Larch Creek*
Wildfire on the Skagit*

The Night Stalkers
MAIN FLIGHT
The Night Is Mine
I Own the Dawn
Wait Until Dark
Take Over at Midnight
Light Up the Night
Bring On the Dusk
By Break of Day

AND THE NAVY
Christmas at Steel Beach
Christmas at Peleliu Cove
WHITE HOUSE HOLIDAY
Daniel's Christmas*
Frank's Independence Day*
Peter's Christmas*
Zachary's Christmas*
Roy's Independence Day*
Damien's Christmas*
5E
Target of the Heart
Target Lock on Love
Target of Mine
Target of One's Own

Shadow Force: Psi
At the Slightest Sound*
At the Quietest Word*

White House Protection Force
Off the Leash*
On Your Mark*
In the Weeds*

Contemporary Romance

Eagle Cove
Return to Eagle Cove
Recipe for Eagle Cove
Longing for Eagle Cove
Keepsake for Eagle Cove

Henderson's Ranch
Nathan's Big Sky*
Big Sky, Loyal Heart*
Big Sky Dog Whisperer*

Love Abroad
Heart of the Cotswolds: England
Path of Love: Cinque Terre, Italy

Other works by M. L. Buchman:

Contemporary Romance (cont)

Where Dreams
Where Dreams are Born
Where Dreams Reside
Where Dreams Are of Christmas
Where Dreams Unfold
Where Dreams Are Written

Science Fiction / Fantasy

Deities Anonymous
Cookbook from Hell: Reheated
Saviors 101

Single Titles
The Nara Reaction
Monk's Maze
the Me and Elsie Chronicles

Non-Fiction

Strategies for Success
Managing Your Inner Artist/Writer
Estate Planning for Authors
Character Voice

Short Story Series by M. L. Buchman:

Romantic Suspense

Delta Force
Delta Force

Firehawks
The Firehawks Lookouts
The Firehawks Hotshots
The Firebirds

The Night Stalkers
The Night Stalkers
The Night Stalkers 5E
The Night Stalkers CSAR
The Night Stalkers Wedding Stories

US Coast Guard
US Coast Guard

White House Protection Force
White House Protection Force

Contemporary Romance

Eagle Cove
Eagle Cove

Henderson's Ranch
Henderson's Ranch

Where Dreams
Where Dreams

Thrillers

Dead Chef
Dead Chef

Science Fiction / Fantasy

Deities Anonymous
Deities Anonymous

Other
The Future Night Stalkers
Single Titles

SIGN UP FOR M. L. BUCHMAN'S
NEWSLETTER TODAY

and receive:
Release News
Free Short Stories
a Free Book

Get your free book today. Do it now.
free-book.mlbuchman.com